Embers of the Heart

A HILLARD FAMILY SAGA

Aimee Collings

ISBN 979-8-89309-469-5 (Paperback)
ISBN 979-8-89309-470-1 (Digital)

Covenant Books
11661 Hwy 707
Murrells Inlet, SC 29576
www.covenantbooks.com

I would like to dedicate this book to my family, my Husband Bryan who has been a constant cheerleader from the sidelines. Allowing me the time to chase my dreams. To my beautiful daughters Harlee and Baylee for being my avid readers and for loving books as much as I do. And to my handsome sons Kyler, Brighton, Camron, and Easton for always supporting their momma and being four of my biggest fans. I am grateful beyond belief for all seven of you. And to my Grandma Karola, thank you for loving me, and accepting me into your family without hesitation. I love you all.

Anna reached for her quilt and pulled it tighter around her chin, pressing her Bible to her chest beneath the blanket with her other hand. She hated this town, but here she was, stuck. She had high hopes for possibly a teaching job, thanks to her schooling in New York. She had attended the best school money could buy. She had thrived as a student and enjoyed learning about faraway places. She had dreams of England and India. How had she ended up in southwest Montana? She knew the answer; she hated that she had to admit her parents were right. She had fallen head over heels for Harold Wilson.

He was eight years her senior. He was tall, dark, and mysterious. He had a smile that melted her into a puddle. Against her parents' wishes, she married Harold. Oh, how she wished she could make a different choice now. Now here she was in a small town full of saloons, drunken men, and a giant lack of womenfolk. And she hadn't heard from her parents in years. When Harold died, she thought she might die too. She had gone days without food. She stopped keeping track when she became too weak to care. Thankfully, she had been stumbled upon by a neighbor returning a horse that had eventually freed itself from the small corral and wandered onto his farm.

Mr. Turner had brought her back to his farm; Mrs. Turner had helped her regain her strength. She stayed for a few short weeks, then saddled her horse and rode away. She had no intention of looking back. She was going to head back east, try to find her sister Sara, and live out her life as a spinster. She had been married to a man who had become quite the actor. In fact, everything she thought she had known about Harold had been a lie—a lie to cover up his real life. She had been promised a nice home, children, and safety that only he could provide for her. He had lied. He was a gambler, not a businessman. He had promised to love and cherish her. Instead, he used his hands to control her.

She had learned quickly to fear him. When he told her of his plans to head west, she had agreed out of fear. He again promised her a wonderful life; she had wanted so badly to believe him. Then he died. He had fallen into the river, through the ice. She had gotten him out, but days later, she assumed pneumonia had set in. She tried to do what she thought was best. She failed; he died only days after the rattling in his chest settled in.

She had mourned the life she was promised. She buried him beneath a tree that stood tall behind their small cabin in the woods. It was a beautiful spot; however, it was only out of necessity that she buried him there. The ground was still quite frozen from the long, cold winter. It took every ounce of strength to get the large man buried. Food quickly ran out, even on the meager rations she had allowed herself. She had lost count of the days she had been alone. She would head back east, find her sister because her parents obviously didn't want her back, and she would never open her heart to another man.

Now, however, her only choice was to pray for sleep in the warmth of her room in the hotel that the Widow McCall ran. She burrowed deeper into her bed as the shouts and gunfire rang out outside her window. One of the four saloons was across the street from the hotel, drunken men littered the streets at this time of night, each one staggering in the direction, or at least they hoped, of home. Gold had been discovered in these parts, and each man with the dream of becoming rich had followed the Montana trails to stake their claim.

Anna shuddered; that was what had brought Harold to the Montana territory. She would be more than happy to leave Bannack once she had enough money to do so. She shut her eyes again, prayed again, until she slipped into a restless sleep.

*****

The next morning, the sun shone bright, and the birds sang a beautiful tune from the trees. Anna eased out of bed and straight to the washbasin of cool water. She splashed the water on her face, begging the permanent darkened circles under her eyes to lighten. She needed to look her best as she searched for a job. She needed a means to take care of herself. Widow McCall had allowed her to stay on, working and cleaning for her. She had a room and sufficient meals; now she needed money. After helping with breakfast and cleanup, she was assigned two rooms that needed a thorough cleaning; then the laundry needed to be hung out to dry. She then headed to the general store looking for a job. Maybe she could check in with the bakery in town as well as the bank. Someone was bound to need help.

She eased her way down the street, tiptoeing her way around the mud and horse droppings that dotted the street. She was greeted by a few men who passed her by, some who stared way too long. She knew she looked out of place. She was raised as a city girl. She had always had the best of everything. From her boots to her fashionable dresses, she looked nothing like the ladies around town, mainly because she was only one of a handful of ladies who didn't work in the saloons. Those ladies hiked their skirts up just a bit too high, wore their necklines just a bit too low, and painted their lips and faces.

Anna had been offered a job working for Bob Rollins at the Wild Horn Saloon, but she hadn't brought herself to that point yet. She was desperate, yes, but not quite that desperate. She would keep trying to find employment elsewhere. Walking into the general store, Jeb Taylor welcomed her.

"Good morning, Mrs. Wilson. Fine morning today has turned out to be. I think spring has finally shown its welcomed face to us yet."

Anna agreed. "I couldn't agree more, Mr. Taylor."

He nodded his head. "What can an old fellow like me do for a lady like yourself today?"

He knew; she knew he knew, but she proceeded anyway. "Still looking for a job, Mr. Taylor." She paused. "Do you happen to know anyone looking for a nanny? Housekeeper? A companion to any of the elderly widows?"

She hoped she didn't look as desperate as she sounded. Mr. Taylor looked at her carefully. "I am right sorry, Mrs. Wilson. I haven't heard a thing. But I'll be more than happy to send anyone looking to your doorstep."

She looked at him with pleading eyes. She knew that next week, and probably the week after, she would get the same answer from him. This town didn't have a lot of extra money to hire extra help. She knew her only real choice was to talk to Mr. Rollins; she just hadn't brought herself to that point. She pushed that thought from her head; she couldn't.

Mr. Taylor asked her if he could do anything else for her. She shook her head no, then bade him farewell as the tears stung at the back of her eyes. She needed to do something. She turned to leave and hurried through the door, running into the chest of a man. She shifted her eyes to the ground, not daring to look up to allow a stranger to see her tears.

"I am sorry, sir." She hurried in the direction of the hotel.

"Pardon me, ma'am," Seth Hillard called to the lady who had just run from the store. She had surprised him and, quite honestly, about knocked him off his feet. He had reached back to grab Tommy, his nine-year-old son, at just the last second before she had collided with the young boy. Thankfully, Mary, his seven-year-old daughter, stood behind him, cradling Beth in her arms. The baby was four months old and would have screamed for the whole town to hear had she taken the force of the woman. If he hadn't known better, he would guess that she had been in tears, which brought him around to the man standing at the counter writing in his books. "Ole Jeb, do I even want to know what you did to that poor woman who just ran out of your establishment?"

Jeb turned toward the door. "Seth! My boy! It's been too long. What, five, six months since you have come to town?"

Seth smiled. "Not quite that long, Jeb, I came right after the passing of Elizabeth."

Four months, Seth thought to himself.

He had hated town; Elizabeth had loved their monthly trips to town. Seth had hated each and every trip. This town had been quite a welcoming place not long ago. Seth remembered the first time Elizabeth and he had stopped at the general store. Elizabeth had been in the family way; they had traveled from about thirty miles south where Grasshopper Creek and the Beaverhead River joined.

In all, they had traveled upward of forty-five miles with a small herd of cows he had spent every last dollar on. He was coming to ask for the mercy of the storekeeper to allow a stranger some credit until he could sell the calves in the fall.

Jeb had become like a father to Seth. The only bright side of coming to town was visiting with Jeb. The townspeople had only stared at him and Elizabeth when they came every month. Elizabeth acted as though her family were strangers to her. The looks of pity were more than he could handle most trips; it took every ounce of self-control not to buy himself a drink or two at the saloon.

"I am in need of some help, Jeb, I was wondering if there might be an old widow in town? Someone to help me raise these youngsters. Between the babe and these two." Seth hooked his finger toward the two children staring at a jar of lemon drops. "I don't have time to run the ranch. As much as Cook and the other men have stepped in to help, it never seems enough."

Jeb nodded his head while he reached for the jar of lemon drops. Grabbing four, he leaned forward to place them in Tommy's hand, looking in Seth's direction for a nod of approval. Seth silently nodded his head toward the old man, a tooth-gapped smile splitting across his face as he whispered to the children.

"Mary, hand your pa that babe. You and Tommy head out to the bench out front. I need to talk to your pa."

Mary did as she was told and handed baby Beth to him. He rubbed Tommy's head. "Stay close. I won't be long."

Seth watched the children slip out the door. Jeb spoke quietly, "Seth, my boy, you don't want some old widow out at the ranch with you. What if she needs doctoring? What will you do? You live four hours by wagon outside of town in the wilds of Montana."

Seth nodded his head. "Jeb, don't I know it. Unfortunately, Elizabeth's passing has rendered me in great need."

Jeb reached for Seth's shoulder. "I understand, my boy. I raised two youngins' on my own after my Martha passed on. It takes a lot out of a man to lose his wife." Jeb paused. "Seth, my boy, what you need is a wife."

Seth stood motionless at Jeb's words. He hadn't even thought about remarrying. His first marriage wasn't bad, but he wasn't sure he would call it good either. She had wanted children right off when he had thought that maybe they should hold off for a bit to get to know each other a bit better. But he had conceded the argument, and within a year, they welcomed little Tommy to the family. With the birth of Tommy, Seth had found himself overly worried about providing for his family, so he stayed in the fields longer and longer each day. He hardly spoke to Elizabeth when he did return to the house because she had already turned in for the night. Nights turned into weeks, weeks turned into months as Seth struggled to provide for his family; the wedge in his and Elizabeth's marriage carried on. Eventually, she talked him into "one more baby, so Tommy has someone to play with."

He agreed that growing up an only child would be difficult, considering the nearest neighbor was half a day's ride away. He would have no playmates, something that didn't sit well with Seth. After the birth of Mary, the finances seemed to even themselves out, and Seth stayed home longer each day. But after years of hardly speaking to each other, the best he could do was offer friendship to Elizabeth. She seemed quite content with the arrangement and even slept in the children's room with them under the ruse of not wanting to wake him if the children needed her. Seth had not opposed the idea at the time, so eventually, all her belongings were moved into a spare room across from the children's.

Seth gave up trying to be anything more than a friend to his wife. Figured they would just live in comfortable silence for the rest of their years. Unfortunately, within seven short years, he would be a widower with three children who needed him. He knew he probably wouldn't stay single the rest of his life, but even thinking about a wife right now had never crossed his mind. "Jeb, you know as well as I any single lady left in these parts is either single for a reason or has no intention of marrying."

Honestly, Seth had figured if he ever remarried, his new wife would come to him by mail, that being all the rage right now. He had no intention of marrying a saloon gal; he needed better than that for his girls. Jeb nodded his head in agreement, then paused mid-nod. "Seth, what if I told you that I know of a very sweet—very pretty, if I do say so myself—young woman who needs security? One who may marry in name only? One that would make an excellent mother to your brood?" He paused, nodded his head again, and continued, "If I were thirty years younger, I would marry the gal myself. However, chances are she would end up a widow for the second time in just a few short years." He chuckled to himself.

Seth let out a breath he had been holding. He didn't even know he had held it. Where was this elusive woman to be found? "Jeb, where would I find such a lady? Today, might I add, as I plan to haul this brood of mine back out to the ranch as soon as possible. No later than tomorrow."

Jeb smiled again. "Son, you just missed her. She walked out of the store not seconds before you walked in. In fact, you probably passed her on the boardwalk."

So Jeb hadn't seen the poor woman flee from the store. "Are you speaking of the young lady who ran from the store in tears, the one who about knocked me off my feet?"

Jeb looked up. "She was in tears?"

"Yes, Jeb, she was. What did you do to the poor woman?"

Jeb nodded his head again, as if thinking this next word out thoroughly. "Son, she lost her husband not but a few months ago. From what I hear, she fled their cabin as soon as she was well enough to do so. He left her to all but starve. He wasn't a good man, even though I don't like speaking ill of the dead. I heard she was happy to see him go. He treated her poorly, you see. She has been searching for work ever since. Bill has invited her to work as a saloon girl multiple times." He stopped to take a breath. "She is a God-fearing woman, Seth. She wouldn't take the job, so instead she comes in here every week, asking around about jobs."

Silence hung about the men for a few short minutes before Seth asked where she could be found. "She is staying at the hotel with Widow McCall. I believe she works off her room and meals."

Seth turned toward the door after handing Jeb a list of supplies he would be taking with him tomorrow. "Her name's Mrs. Anna Wilson!" Jeb yelled to him before the door closed.

*****

Anna hurried her entire way home, keeping her head down to avoid as many stares as possible. Once she reached the hotel, she slipped inside, hoping to make it to her room to put herself to rights. She pulled her door closed and sank into the chair next to the door. She needed to make a plan. She couldn't live like this forever. She needed a reason, a purpose. Under Harold's watchful eye, she had spent the last four years scurrying around her husband, staying quiet and out of his way. She made meals and cleaned up what she could before it made him angry. She felt broken, and living in a small room with a chair, bed, and chest was not what she had in mind for the rest of her life. She needed to make money; unfortunately, it seemed the only way she was going to be making any money was by taking the job as a saloon girl. The thought of that gave her a bad taste in her mouth. The smell of alcohol reminded her so much of Harold and his anger that she became physically ill just thinking about it. She couldn't do it; she wouldn't do it.

*****

Seth loaded the kids back into the wagon and headed toward the south end of town. In the back of the wagon, Mary sweetly hummed a tune to Beth to keep her happy. Tommy straightened his shoulders and peered out the side of the wagon. The boy had always been so happy, so full of life. Now he was almost a shell of himself. He smiled here and there, but the smile never quite reached his eyes. He had stopped playing and had taken up sitting and watching his sisters play. It broke Seth's heart. He needed his little boy back; if getting married would fix whatever Tommy needed fixing, then Seth would do it. He would do anything for his children. Seth's mind wandered while the wagon rolled down the muddy road. Could he actually go through with a marriage to a stranger? Could he expect a woman to marry him, a man with three children? She had to have other offers. Single ladies didn't go unnoticed around here. She must have plenty of attention from the men in town.

It took everything in him to keep the wagon rolling toward the hotel. *I could finish my shopping and head back home*, he thought to himself. *But the children. Little Beth looked plum worn out I cannot do that to them.* His eyes jolted his mind back to the reality of his situation. He needed help with the children, be it a wife or an old widow. A wife? Could he remarry? Could he live with another woman as just her friend? Didn't he deserve more? And the lady whom he would marry, wouldn't she deserve more as well? Too late, the wagon was now rolling to a stop outside the hotel, and a young man named Peter jumped from the boardwalk.

"Mornin', Mr. Hillard!"

"Good morning, Peter."

"Let me take care of the horses and wagon, Mr. Hillard. I'll take right good care of it for you."

"I know you will, Peter. I appreciate it."

Seth then turned to the kids, grabbed Beth, and held out a hand for Mary. Tommy grabbed the carpet bag that contained all their clothing.

Seth had planned on making a few extra stops before heading to the hotel, but with this marriage thing hanging over his head, he figured it best to address that problem first, then address the lumber mill, blacksmith, and post office. When Seth opened the door to the hotel, the smell of fresh-baked goods assaulted his nose. Oh how he had missed Elizabeth's baked goods. She loved to bake as much as she loved the kids, he dared guess, and it showed. Her sugar cookies all but melted in his mouth.

"Make yourself at home, I'll be right there," was shouted from the kitchen.

Seth smiled to himself. Widow McCall was as dear to him as Ole Jeb. She had taken him and Elizabeth in when they first arrived in town. She had proven to be a good friend over the years to both Elizabeth and himself.

"Seth! Tommy, Mary, Beth! Oh, my!" She pulled her hands up to cover her mouth. Tears stung her eyes.

He hadn't realized how much he had missed her until now. Seth walked quickly to her side. "Hello, Helen, sorry I have been away so long. I have had my hands quite full as of late."

Helen squeezed his arm then reached for the baby. "Oh my sweet little Beth, look at you! You look just like your pa." As she settled the baby into her arms, she shifted her eyes toward the other two kids. "Are you two going to come give your aunt Helen a hug? Or am I going to have to beg?"

Both kids raced to her side and wrapped their small arms about her waist.

"Seth, what has brought you to town this morning? I can't even imagine what time you woke these poor babies up to be here so early in the day. They all could probably use some refreshments and a nap."

Just then, both Mary and Beth yawned, which brought a smile to Seth's face. He knew Helen would take them now, and he was grateful for the small break. He loved those children, but between them and the ranch, he was worn out. Having a loving woman step in and take them for a few short minutes was a blessing in his book. "Seth, go put your bag in room six, end of the hall up the stairs. We'll meet you in the kitchen."

Seth nodded and climbed the stairs two at a time. Once inside the room, he heard a door down the hall open and then close; the soft sound of small boots reached his ears. He peeked out the door but saw no one. So he shut the door, walked to the water basin, washed his hands and face, and headed back out of the door.

*****

Anna heard lots of noise coming from the kitchen, so she headed that way. She knew it wasn't time to make the midday meal, but Helen was definitely up to something. She figured she better see if the older woman needed any help. As she neared the door, she heard the soft sound of a small baby cry; Anna stopped for a heartbeat and listened again. "It's okay, sweet girl, your pa will be right back to hold you," she heard Helen say.

Anna continued through the door and stopped just inside. Three sets of eyes turned her direction, and a bundle in Helen's arms squirmed and let out another unhappy cry. Helen was trying to pour milk into two cups, but with the handful she was currently holding, she was struggling. Anna reached her in two long strides. "How can I help?" she asked Helen.

"Umm, hold the baby, please. Then I will be able to feed those two a quick snack."

Helen held the baby out to Anna. Anna had not held a baby in years. She was grateful she had never found herself in the family way while Harold was alive. She hated to even think about bringing a baby into that home. She grabbed the baby and pulled her to her chest. "Well, hello, little one, and what is your name, sweetheart?"

"Beth," three voices rang out at once.

That brought a smile to Anna's face. "And you are?" looking at the two other children.

"My name is Tommy. This is my sister, Mary."

"Well, hello, Tommy, Mary, and Beth. It's very nice to meet you. My name is Anna."

"Nice to meet you too, ma'am," Tommy said behind his glass of milk.

Mary had already taken a drink and was now the proud owner of an adorable milk mustache.

Anna turned her face back to the bundle in her arms. "And Miss Beth, how old might you be?"

"Four months, almost five," a fifth voice said behind her.

Anna jumped a little and turned around, coming face-to-face with the darkest brown eyes she had ever seen. Those brown eyes belonged to a man just taller than herself, with broad strong shoulders and sun-kissed skin. A short, well-kept beard covered his face that reached up to his dark brown hair. Anna shifted slightly to the side to let him pass. When he didn't move, she tried to find her voice. "Hello, I am guessing you are the pa that Mrs. McCall just spoke of."

Seth nodded his head. "That I am. My name is Seth Hillard. Nice to meet you, Mrs. Wilson."

Anna's eyebrows shot up. "Forgive me, sir, have we met?"

Seth smiled a perfect smile. "No, ma'am, not exactly. I happened to be walking into the general store this morning while you were walking out."

"Oh," Anna mouthed, "I am sorry about that, sir, I hadn't meant to run into you like that. I was in quite a hurry."

"Seth, everyone calls me Seth. Unless they work for me, then it's Boss man or Mr. Hillard. Everyone else calls me Seth."

Anna looked from him to Helen, who nodded her approval.

"Then I shall be Anna." At that moment, the baby reached her small arm out of the blanket and grabbed at Anna's face. She turned to look down at the baby. Seth took a second to look in the direction of his children and Helen, who had now begun a conversation about a new foal that was out in her barn. The kids asked question after question about the foal, chickens, and kittens. Seth turned back to Anna; she was playing with the baby. Beth cooed at Anna.

"Oh really, Miss Beth, and then what happened?" Anna asked the baby, with a smile plastered on her face.

Seth set his eyes on the woman before him. To be honest, she was one of the most beautiful ladies he had ever seen. Her long blonde hair, only pulled partway away from her face, fell in curls down her back. Her green eyes sparkled with happiness. Her pale skin looked as though it was made of cream. When she smiled, it reached her eyes; her giggle filled the room with joy. Seth turned back toward his children. "Tommy, Mary, will you please take Beth up to the room? I have a few things I need to talk to Aunt Helen and Mrs. Anna about."

Tommy nodded his head. "I'll put them down for a nap, Pa."

Then he turned to Mary. "Come along, Mary."

Seth shook his head as his son reached up to grab the bundle wrapped in Anna's arms. "I'll take her, Mrs. Anna."

Then the children disappeared through the door.

"May we go to the sitting room, Helen?" Seth asked.

Helen nodded her head and motioned for Anna to lead the way. Seth brought up the rear and took the seat just opposite Anna's and next to Helen's. Seth had always been a man to speak what was on his mind, yet at this very moment, he couldn't seem to get his brain to work with his mouth to speak the words he intended to say. Helen looked at Seth while Anna looked to Helen for answers. "Seth, son, if you have something to say, I sure wish you would do it. You are making my insides crawl."

Seth looked toward Helen. "I am sorry, Helen, I need to get this right, so I am trying to find my words. I am sorry for making you uncomfortable." Seth sighed, then continued, "Anna, I am in need of a caretaker for my children and my home. I need someone to school them, play with them, and teach them what their mother could not. I need someone to help make meals and help with the house. As I am sure you have heard, my wife passed just after the birth of Beth. She has never known a mother. My other two children have been heartbroken since she left us." He stopped and looked into her eyes. Would he be able to read what she was thinking? "I understand what I am asking is a lot, but it cannot be helped. I need a wife."

Out of the corner of his eye, he saw Helen raise a hand to her heart. Her eyes glistened with tears, so he shifted his attention to her and reached for her hand. "I am sorry this has upset you, Helen, that was not my intention."

Then he turned back to Anna. "I understand this is a lot to think about, Anna. I did not mean for this trip into town to go this way. I will only return every six months or so, so I would need your answer now so we can marry in the morning before I have to head back to the ranch."

Anna's breath caught in her lungs. Had he just proposed to her? Was she meant to answer now? She was pretty sure he had said something about that, but she was finding it difficult to focus on what he was saying. "Sir, are you asking me to wed you tomorrow?"

She cut him off. He stopped talking. "Yes, ma'am, I am. My children need a mother. I can take care of you. You won't need or want for anything. I own and run the largest cattle ranch in southwest Montana. I will be caring and keep you safe."

Her eyes shifted from his to Helen, who still held his hand. Helen finally looked in her direction and nodded. Was that an approval? *Is she nodding to me to say yes?* Anna shifted her eyes back to Seth. His eyes bore into her soul. She blinked, but when she reopened her eyes, he still looked at her with the darkest eyes she had ever seen. She froze. What was she supposed to say? She knew what he wanted her to say, even Helen. But how did she trust herself to live under the same roof as a man again? The last time hadn't worked out very well.

She stood from the couch and made her way toward the door. She needed to think and think fast, when a hand reached out for hers. She looked down at the large, calloused hand, then up to the owner's face. Seth stood close enough she could feel his breath brush its way across her face. She looked into those dark eyes again and saw what she could only assume was need. He did not break eye contact with her, which set her insides on fire, not to mention the heat running up her arm from his touch. "I am sorry, Anna. I cannot imagine what you are thinking. But I promise to be a good, noble, honest, and harmless husband to you."

He stopped speaking again and took a small step toward her. "I will not hurt you, Anna. I have never hurt a lady ever in my twenty-eight years of life. I have no plans to start now."

Anna nodded her head, then excused herself.

Anna walked to the kitchen and out the door to the back of the house. Tears burned in her eyes for the second time today. Her hands shook at her sides, her insides trembled. How? And why? Who had told him of her husband's treatment of her? Her stomach flipped, and she felt sick. The thought of living under another man's roof made her tremble over and over. Tears streamed down her face at a rapid pace. She felt the need to run, yet her legs wouldn't allow it. So caught up in her thoughts, she hadn't heard the door open and close softly behind her. "He's a good man, Anna," Helen said from behind her, making her jump.

"Helen! You scared me!" She paused to catch her breath and wipe away the tears that slipped down her face. "I don't know what he wants from me, Helen. I don't know the man. It would be one thing if he wanted to court and get to know me." She paused, steadied her breathing, and started again. "He is a stranger, Helen, a stranger who wants me to marry him and live in the woods for the next six months alone. He could hurt me." She paused again. "or worse," she said under her breath.

Helen eased an arm around Anna's arm and pulled her close. Helen had become Anna's closest and only friend here in town. She knew without a doubt Helen would never harm her or place her in harm's way. "Anna, I have known Seth for near on a decade. He would never hurt you. I would never stand by and watch him hurt you. He has worked endless hours to become a wealthy man. He will not leave you to need or want for anything. Elizabeth, God rest her soul, lived an extremely comfortable life with Seth. If he is asking for help now, it is only because he needs it." She paused. "Did you see those babies? Anna, you need a way out of this town. Those children need a mother." Helen stopped to look Anna in the eye. "I wouldn't hesitate if I were you. A man like that comes but once in a lifetime."

Helen then turned and walked back toward the house. Anna sat frozen to the spot. Helen was encouraging her to accept his hand? She sat on a nearby stump, placed her head in her hands, and cried some more. She was terrified.

Seth let go of Anna's hand, warmth still stole up his arm. He stared at where she stood. He turned to Helen, tipped his head, and walked out of the room himself. He climbed the stairs slowly. His head was spinning. This was not in his plans for the day. He wanted to find an older lady who could be somewhat of a grandma to his children, helping and teaching them. He needed someone to hold the baby while he was working with the cattle or on his horse, Dollar. He wanted to still be with his children most of the day, but he needed help.

An older lady would have been easier. He wouldn't need to marry her. Anna was young, he guessed close to twenty-five, and therefore, they would have to marry to remain proper. He would never even think to take her with him unwed to her. Had he made the right decision? He didn't know, but he felt awful for causing so much trouble.

When he made it to his room, the two girls lay cuddled together in the middle of the bed, while Tommy lay along the foot of the bed. All three sound asleep. His heart broke all over again. Elizabeth was a fantastic mother most days; she wasn't what he had wanted or expected in a wife. However, over the years, they had grown fond of each other. When she died, it was like a piece of his puzzle died, but not necessarily his heart. He had grown to love Elizabeth as family should love, but he was not in love with her. He hated himself for not caring any more for the mother of his children, but she had made it perfectly clear to him that her heart belonged elsewhere. He had never told anyone about that particular conversation they had had. He kept that locked in the dark edges of his heart that nobody would ever see.

She had told him of a man named Quincy Morgan whom she had loved all her life. He had been forced into an unwanted marriage, so with Quincy married to another, the heartbroken Elizabeth set her sights on Seth. He was in no hurry to marry, but she had ignored his reservations. Apparently, her father caught wind of them spending a "long time at night alone together"; it hadn't happened, but Seth was man enough to make it right. He married her three days later. Sometimes he strongly believed she had only married him to have children. She needed to love someone other than Quincy, so she had Tommy, then Mary, and then Beth. She loved them all fiercely. He had been so grateful for the love and kindness she had shown the kids he chose to forget about the feelings she kept from him. Not that he had offered her any of those feelings either. "Comfortable" would sum up their lives together.

Not wanting to wake the babies, Seth hustled to the kitchen to speak with Helen. He needed to run a few more errands before he left town tomorrow morning. After talking to Helen and asking her if she wouldn't mind listening for the children to wake up, he slipped out the front door and walked back toward the center of town.

Not quite an hour after Seth walked out the door, Beth started to fuss. Helen asked Anna to go and grab her, using her swollen knee as an excuse for not wanting to walk up the stairs. Anna shook her head and headed up to the room. She slowly opened the door, trying not to wake the other two children. Once Beth saw her, she cooed and flapped her arms about. Anna reached her quickly and wrapped her in a blanket, then headed back down the stairs with the babe.

Helen handed her a bottle of warm cow's milk. She sat in a rocking chair and held the baby close, feeding the baby while rocking her eased the tension in her muscles. Once Beth finished her bottle, Anna placed the small child against her shoulder to burp her. Anna laughed out loud when Beth let out quite a large burp for such a small little thing.

"Well, Miss Beth, you must feel all better now, don't you?" Anna said with laughter in her voice.

Beth cooed again at her, then lifted her hand again to Anna's face. Anna smiled and continued to talk to the baby like they had known each other for years. Anna lifted the child up to rub her nose against her own, and Beth cooed again. Anna's smile lightened her whole face. This child had stolen her heart. Her big brown eyes she now stared up at her with looked just like her father's, just a touch lighter. Her brown fuzzy hair stood on its end and looked just adorable on the round face that was now smiling up at her.

Anna's own smile couldn't be helped. Movement out of the corner of her eye caught her attention. She looked up to stare at the matching set of eyes as the babe in her arms. She felt her stomach flip. The room wasn't quite spinning but not standing still either. They stared at each other for more than a few short seconds when the baby laid her head against Anna's chest and cooed to herself. That brought Seth's eyes to the baby, then back to her.

Her heart froze while she waited to see if he was going to say something to her or not. Did he want an answer? She wasn't entirely sure what that answer was going to be, so she hoped not. Seth moved toward her, his eyes fixed on her until he reached her, then his eyes shifted to the baby in her arms, and he reached out and lifted the child from her. He thanked her for keeping her for him while he took care of the other needs he had planned to fill while in town and disappeared up the stairs. She stared in his direction until she heard the door to his room shut softly behind him. Then she turned her eyes to her now empty arms.

Her body trembled from deep inside again. She tried to focus on her feelings, but she couldn't. She was picturing the motherless and wifeless family up the stairs. She pushed herself upright and walked into the kitchen. She needed to wash the baby's bottle and help prepare supper. Helen stood at the stove, just getting ready to slide a batch of rolls into the oven. She paused and looked over her shoulder, then continued with her task. "Where did our sweet Beth go?" Helen asked.

"Seth came back and took her upstairs after she finished her bottle."

Helen nodded her head in understanding and continued her duties.

"How can I help, Helen?" Anna asked cautiously. Anna could see the love Helen held for Seth, so she knew she had probably hurt the woman's feelings when she had assumed he would treat her unkind. Helen hadn't said much to her since they had talked outside.

"Stew and rolls for tonight, cookies for dessert, everything is done, but thank you." Helen looked in the direction of Anna and watched the color drain from her face. "You helped take care of the babe. So you have already helped. If I had to feed that babe, I would have never given her up, so you see you have kept us all from starving tonight, Anna." With that, Helen smiled at her. "We will sit and have a bit of tea if you are up to it while we wait for the rolls to finish cooking."

Anna agreed to the tea and set two cups, the cream pitcher, and the sugar on the table. Then she fetched the tea. The two ladies talked about all sorts of things while they drank their tea. Life here with Helen had become comfortable. Anna had longed for this kind of home her whole life.

Seth heard soft voices trickling from the kitchen. He could smell cookies and fresh coffee. He wasn't about to miss out on that. He held Beth in his arms as the other two slipped past him and into the kitchen. "Aunt Helen!" Mary yelled. "We really want to see your new foal. Can we, please?"

Helen smiled at the children, handed them both a cookie, and motioned toward the back door. The kids whooped as the door opened, and they ran ahead of Helen. Mary's long brown braids, that normally hung down to rest upon her shoulders, now whipped in the wind, and her big blue eyes danced with excitement.

Anna could not remember there ever being a more beautiful child. Then she looked at Tommy. Those same big blue eyes danced as he looked toward Helen, but the blonde, almost yellow hair upon his head looked nothing like the rest of the family. He had very small similarities to Seth, but nothing that would tie him solely to him. *He must have taken after Elizabeth*, she thought to herself.

Seth headed for the stove; the smell of coffee was too inviting for him to not grab a cup. Anna thought about helping him; she could get his coffee for him or maybe taking the baby would be more helpful. She was fighting a war within herself when she heard Seth say something.

"I am sorry, what did you say?"

Seth smiled slightly. "I asked if you would hold her for me while I pour this coffee. I don't want to splash it on her little legs."

Anna jumped to her feet and reached for the baby without hesitation. "Absolutely."

He moved toward her while she moved toward him. Soon they were a breath away from each other, her hands wrapping around the baby, somehow brushing against his. She looked up as warmth spread through her body. Their eyes met, she smiled slightly, and then he turned his head and walked back toward the stove. "Thank you, Anna. It's nice to have some help sometimes."

Anna nodded her head while looking at the baby. "I can't imagine it's hard to find help from any lady when it comes to helping with a baby." Then she clamped her mouth shut along with her eyes and prayed he hadn't heard her.

He chuckled and said, "You have no idea," then he laughed again.

Why had she said that? She shook her head. The inward battle started again. After a long uncomfortable bout of silence, Seth spoke again. "Anna, I appreciate you loving on the children today. You have been helpful with them today, and I appreciate it." He studied her face for a few moments. "I also don't mean to add any pressure to you." He paused again, reformed his words, then continued, "But

I do need an answer to my proposal we talked about earlier today. I will need to call on Reverend Mills if we are to marry tomorrow morning." He studied her face; she looked terrified, but her eyes softened, and he held his breath.

"Seth, this is all so much to take in. You want me to be a mother, a wife, and a housekeeper. I am not sure I am up for the task you have asked me to consider." She locked eyes with him again, and a flash of disappointment appeared in his eyes. Then she continued, "I need to know I will be safe with you. I am scared. You are a stranger to me." A few stray tears slipped down her cheeks.

Seth walked toward her and pulled out the empty chair to face her before he sat down. Their knees brushed against each other, and that same warm feeling ran through her body. "Anna, I don't think my words will be enough for you. I understand Mr. Wilson was unkind and caused you pain. But I can assure you I would never hurt you. I promised God the day Beth was born that if he let her live, I would do everything in my power to be the kind of man he would be proud of. I plan on sticking by that promise because, as you can see, He spared my daughter's life."

Tears again traced down her cheeks; this time, they didn't quite make it down to her lips because Seth reached out with his thumb and wiped them away. When his hand had moved toward her face at first, she almost flinched; then his rough thumb softly touched her cheek and wiped away her tears. He was so gentle with her. Her heart melted just enough to allow her to nod her head. Seth watched her for a second and then asked, "Anna, are you agreeing to marry me, or—"

She cut him off, "Yes, Seth, I will marry you. I am still scared, but I believe God sent you here to me. I will help you raise your children and—"

It was his turn to cut her off, "Our children, Anna, our children."

With that, he stood and then leaned toward her. He placed a soft kiss to her forehead and said he would be back soon, but he really needed to see Reverend Mills.

*****

Upon entering the small church, Anna was met with the dark brown eyes that stayed in her dreams all night. Sleep was useless. She had tried, but every time she closed her eyes, Seth's face, more importantly his eyes, filled her mind. Now standing at the front of the small church, those same eyes locked on hers. She took a very shaky step forward; she could do this. She needed this family as her way out of this town; they needed a mother. Unfortunately, that also made her a wife again. She trembled again. Seth was so far nothing like Harold. He seemed good. She could not remember those feelings toward Harold. He always seemed sneaky, always looking for the next easy win. Now that she was older, she could see it for what it was all along. He always needed money because he always owed someone a substantial amount of money. From racehorses to poker hands, Harold lost money at an extremely fast pace. Moving out west was his way of running from his last victim, she was sure of it.

Now here she was, walking into another marriage. She tried not to cringe at the memories of what that meant. Seth deserved better from her. She had to at least try to do better. She forced a smile and locked eyes again with Seth. She needed his strength to go through with this.

Seth was mesmerized when Anna came through the church doors. She wore a light cream dress that fell beautifully around her. Her blonde hair was knotted on top of her head with beautiful curls hanging about her face. Her green eyes sparkled. Then, as if she remembered what she was doing, a cloud of uncertainty washed over them. Her lips drew into a fine line. She looked as if she were ready to run. Seth hoped not. He didn't know Anna well enough to decide how this marriage was going to pan out. What he did know was that he felt comfortable with her. Her soft smiles at the children gave him hope. And right now, he needed just that.

He kept his eyes focused on his soon-to-be wife and watched her take in everything and everyone but him. He prayed silently that she would find him again. Then she squared her shoulders and raised her head again. Whatever battle she was fighting, she had either just won or she had resigned herself. He hoped it wasn't the latter. She smiled in his direction. But it wasn't that big, beautiful smile she had for his sweet Beth, but he would take a smile. Even a small one; he was grateful, so he offered a quick prayer and smiled back at her.

Other than the children, Helen and Jeb Taylor, the church was empty, which was what both Seth and Anna had agreed upon the night before. Seth stood with his hands clasped behind him. Reverend Mills stood with a Bible in his. Sooner than she possibly thought, she stood next to Seth in front of the reverend, and he began the service. Anna gave a quick "I do" when the reverend addressed her. She heard Seth repeat the same words, then she waited for the moment she was entirely unprepared for.

"Seth, you may kiss your bride."

Seth turned to face Anna, her mouth went dry, and she froze. Seth smiled his perfect smile and leaned toward her. She licked her lips and studied his eyes. He gave her a quick grin after she licked her lips and then turned his eyes to her mouth. Time stood still. His lips felt like feathers. So soft yet strong in a way she didn't quite understand. Her body raged with fire when he pulled away and reached for her hand. Then he brushed his lips against the back of her hand and turned toward the children.

After the excited congratulations, the new family headed out the door to the waiting wagon. Seth had made it perfectly clear he wanted to head for home as soon as possible. He had asked Anna to bring her belongings with her to the church even. What she had wasn't much. A small bag with three dresses and one nightdress wasn't hard to pack the night before. She reached for the bag when Seth reached around her and grabbed it himself, a soft, small smile on his face. "Allow me, Mrs. Hillard."

She offered a smile in return. Seth talked to the reverend for a few minutes while Anna spoke to Helen. Helen reassured her of what good fortune she had, went on and on about what a "good and fine man" Seth was.

Once all their goodbyes had been spoken, Seth lifted Mary into the back of the wagon, took the baby from Anna, and offered her his hand up. Once she was settled onto the seat, he handed her Beth. Tommy climbed into the wagon by way of the wheel, and Seth walked around the front of the horses, giving them one last inspection before he climbed up to sit next to Anna on the bench. Jeb Taylor yelled out that he would meet them at the general store to grab the supplies Seth had ordered, and they were off.

The wagon rocked and bounced with each rock, hole, and rut that the wheels hit; Anna found herself pressed against Seth's side more than once. Each touch set a sliver of heat rushing through her body. She had to focus her attention on keeping herself upright in order to keep Beth from being tossed about. Once they reached the lumber mill, Seth turned in her direction. "We are wanting to add a room or two to the house. I need to arrange the delivery real quick, are you okay to wait here?"

Anna, who had never been thought of nor concerned for by any man other than her father, whom she had let terribly down, just stared at Seth. His look of concern finally brought her back to what he had just said. "Of course, we will be fine, won't we, children?"

Both children bobbed their heads. Seth took another quick look at Anna and jumped down to the muddy road below. "I'll be but a minute." Then he walked away.

Mary reached for Beth, asking if she could sing to and play with the baby. While Tommy watched his father disappear into the small building, Anna watched him carefully while she handed the baby back to Mary. "Tommy, I bet if you hurry in, you will get a chance to be a part of whatever it is you men find so fascinating about lumber. You better go quick!"

Tommy turned to her with a smile that reached his eyes and then some. Then as quickly as it showed up, it faded away, but he bounded out of the wagon and into the open door. Anna hoped she wasn't overstepping. What she did know of Seth was that he loved his children dearly, so she hoped that he wouldn't mind the young boy being underfoot while talking business. The smile that had changed that boy's face in just a few mere seconds would be worth whatever anger Seth gave her, she decided. That was the first of what she hoped would be many smiles that Tommy offered her; it was worth it.

Mary sang the sweetest little tune to Beth. Anna found herself with her eyes closed, just listening to the girls, when she heard footsteps heading her way. She jerked her eyes open to look straight into the eyes of her new husband. He didn't necessarily look angry, but he wasn't very happy. Tommy climbed back into the wagon just as Seth plopped himself next to her. She shifted her eyes to her hands and prepared for the anger to spill out of Seth. He took a deep breath and turned to her. *Here it is*, she thought. *This man won't even wait until we are in our own home.* He would let her have whatever it was he was going to give her right here on the streets of Bannack.

"I tell you what!"

She took a deep breath, begging him with her eyes not to say or do anything to her in front of the children. "That—" Then he stopped. His face was full of confusion; his eyes showed worry. "Anna, is something wrong?" He reached for her hand. She flinched, and he pulled away. "Anna, has something happened just now?"

She looked at him as tears started to form in her eyes. With a trembling voice, she said, "I am sorry, Seth. He wanted so badly to come with you." She rushed through her words. Maybe if she could tell him the reason she had allowed Tommy to go with his father, he wouldn't be as upset with her. "He looked so sad. I didn't mean to cause trouble, I was just trying to gain his trust. Please don't be angry with him. It was all my fault, I shall—"

Seth stopped her by placing one finger to her lips. He wasn't angry with her. He didn't know Tommy wanted to go or he would have offered to take him in the first place. He figured he had one of two options to get her to stop talking long enough for him to let her know as such. One, place a finger to her mouth; two, well—he smiled inwardly—would be to kiss her. He had always watched his own pa do just that when his ma was rambling on about something. It always seemed to work too. Maybe one day he would try that. Today, he would use his finger to stop her words.

Under his finger, he felt her tremble. He used his thumb to wipe away the one lone tear that slipped down her cheek. "Anna, sweetheart, I am not angry with you or with Tommy. I should have taken the boy myself. He does not bother me one bit. I am upset with Mr. Scott. Yesterday, he offered one price, today he wants another. Crooked men are not people I like to deal with. Thankfully, I talked some sense into the man, considering I was already willing to pay quite a high price for delivery and all."

When Seth stopped speaking, Anna turned her eyes back to her folded hands and quietly mumbled, "I am sorry, Seth. I didn't mean to accuse you."

He slowly grabbed her chin and turned her face back toward his. "Anna, you have nothing to apologize for. It was a simple misunderstanding." With that, he turned to the horses, released the brake, and urged the horses forward.

Anna felt horrible; she had been married for what? An hour? And she was already causing problems for her new husband. The problem was that seemed to be the only thing she was good at when it came to marriage. If she had ever had any doubts about that, Harold was more than happy to inform her of it. Now here she was again, doing the same thing to another man. She needed to learn to hold her tongue, do her chores, and stay out of the way. Things worked better that way. They made a stop at the bakery for a few goods to give the children on their way home, then they stopped at the general store.

Everyone climbed down from the wagon. Once Seth helped Anna down, and she grabbed the baby so Mary could climb down, Seth placed his hand on Anna's back and guided them into the store. The feeling of his hand on her back sent her mind swimming. Harold had never shown her kindness after their marriage. The feel of his hand on her was normally accompanied by pain. To have a man's hand linger on her back or hips the way Seth's had was completely foreign to her. She tried not to let her thoughts show as they moved toward the counter.

Jeb stood as proud as a peacock as he watched the new family approach him. "Man alive, if it isn't the most handsome family in town. If I didn't know better, I would never have guessed y'all just tied the knot." He smiled again.

Seth smiled at the old man. "I won't argue with you, Jeb."

Anna smiled at the old man. "Thank you, Jeb."

Mary slipped her hand into Anna's and started pulling on her arm. "Papa says I can call you Anna or Ma. I wanna call you Ma, if that's all right with you."

Anna nodded at her and smiled. "I like the sound of that, sweet girl."

"Good," Mary said. "Now that I have a ma again, you are going to want your baby back. So I would like a baby of my own. This one!"

Mary held up a doll that looked an awful lot like her sister with big brown eyes and brown curls on top. "Oh, Mary, that doll is beautiful, but—" She felt Seth's hand on her arm.

"You know what, Mary?" he said. "You and Tommy have been so much help with Beth, I think you both deserve a reward. You may have the doll, Mary. Tommy, you may also pick out a new toy if you'd like." Then he squeezed Anna's arm gently. "I would also like for you to pick out a new outfit or something for the baby, as well as a new coat, boots, and dress for yourself, and"—he paused—"anything else you might need." He nodded his head toward the underclothes and nightclothes against the back wall.

"Seth, that is too much. The expense would be too great. I am in no need of new clothing. I will mend what I can and I will manage."

Seth's smile stopped her in her tracks. "Anna, either you can pick out what you like or I can do it for you. Either way, you are getting a few new dresses." He looked at the dresses that hung nearby. "I think that green one right there would look beautiful on you." Then as fast as he had shown up, he turned to walk away. "I will just be loading up our goods if you need me to pick out your new coat as well." Then he turned and winked at her.

Her heart stopped. After locating the boots, she found that each of the kids was getting close to needing a new pair as well. So she grabbed them both a pair as well as a pair for herself. She found the coats easy enough and found a dark green just a shade darker than the new dress she had picked up. The second dress she chose was a dark blue skirt with a cream top. The underclothes would be a blessing. It had been quite some time since she had gotten any new ones. She also grabbed a few bolts of fabric. Something to make a few new clothes for each child, including the baby, as well as a few colors she thought she could make Seth a few new shirts out of.

Tommy grabbed a wooden horse to go along with Mary's new doll, and they walked to the counter with more than she thought. While staring at the pile of goods she placed on the counter, she paled at the cost. She started to add the cost in her mind. It was too great. She reached for the blue dress and boots to go put them back. Seth stepped up beside her in that moment and said, "Oh, maybe this blue one will look even better than the green. I doubt it, but maybe." He smiled. "Excellent choice." And he placed them back on the counter.

Anna watched him as he turned toward Jeb. He really was a handsome man. And kind. She needed to remind herself of that. In the twenty-four hours she had known Seth, he had already shown her more kindness than in the four years she was married to Harold. Honestly, she didn't know what to do with a kind man. "What's the damage, ole man?" Seth asked.

Anna about fainted on the spot when Jeb finished adding everything up. She almost fainted again when Seth pulled the money out of his pocket and paid the man on the spot. She hadn't had that luxury in quite a few years. Seth and Tommy loaded up their arms, Jeb followed them to the wagon with a wooden crate full of goods, while Mary ran ahead with her new doll, and Anna snuggled the baby.

Once everyone was back and settled, the wagon lurched forward again. Seth turned back toward the children. "Y'all ready to get back home?"

Tommy smiled, the second smile today. It warmed Anna's heart. Mary nodded with enthusiasm. Seth turned to her next and reached over to grab Beth's tiny foot. He smiled at his sweet baby. Beth had been the light at the end of a very ugly tunnel for him. He missed Elizabeth, but he got the best from her to keep her on Earth with him. Beth was a gift right from the start.

While pregnant with Beth, Elizabeth had become very ill. They had sent for the doctor more than once a month for the first few months; she couldn't and eventually wouldn't eat. Without any food making it into her already small frame, it didn't take long before she was left completely bedridden. As the months dragged on, she seemed to fall further and further away from her family. The children were always too loud or shut the door too hard; they played too roughly. Mary would sneak into her room to watch her mother sleep, only to be told to "get out" every time she awoke to the child sitting in the chair at the foot of her bed.

By the time the baby was due to come, Doc Richards didn't think Elizabeth would be able to endure the labor that was soon to be upon them. When labor started, Seth sent one of his hired hands for the doctor. Unfortunately, by the time Doc Richards had made it to the farm, Elizabeth had already endured a very rough labor, and what little energy she had was now spent, and she couldn't muster up the strength to continue. Doc Richards had to shove Seth from the room at the last minute. When he returned to the room a short time later, his wife lay lifeless on the bed, his new baby lay lifeless in the doctor's hands.

Seth stood motionless in the room when Dr. Richards explained to him what had happened. He had lost Elizabeth; he had tried to save her, but her poor exhausted body just couldn't take the strain. She had seen the baby, smiled a weakened smile, closed her eyes, and went to sleep, or so the doctor had thought at first. He worked vigorously on the baby to keep her alive. When he looked back to Elizabeth, she had already passed.

Seth's throat went impossibly dry, taking a breath was all but impossible. He found the closest chair and sat himself in it. His heart was beating like he had just run across the back pasture, not simply walked into a room. Doc Richards handed him the baby and asked for her name. He stared down at one of the three most beautiful babies he had ever seen. She nuzzled into his arms, and he pressed a soft kiss to her brown fluffy hair. "Beth," he whispered against her hair. "Her name is Beth."

*****

Seth snapped from his thoughts to look up at Anna. A small smile reached her lips. He smiled back at her. Here he was on his way home with a new wife and three happy and healthy children. He looked back at the road in front of him and smiled again. He had always considered himself a lucky man; however, today, he thought of himself as an extremely lucky man. He snapped the reins. "Let's go home, boys!"

The wagon moved quickly down the road; a small stream followed them along the trail. After a handful of hours of being tossed around the wagon bench wrapped in Anna's arms, Beth let them all know she had had enough. Seth smiled toward the little bundle. "Okay, little lady, I think it's about time to stop too."

Anna shifted in the seat as well. It had been quite some time since she had sat upon the hard bench of a wagon. Her body was sure to give her fits tomorrow. Seth pulled the wagon into a small cove under the trees next to the stream. Anna turned to the children. "Please stay close and don't go too close to the water."

Seth nodded his head at the children. "She's the boss, children, we all better listen up." Then he winked at her.

She blushed and handed him the baby. Seth helped her off the wagon, and she reached to take the baby again, figuring he needed to tend to the horses. "I've got her, your arms must be tired by now. You go grab the blanket and lunch we brought along, and I'll watch this little lady."

Anna smiled and walked quickly to the back of the wagon. Tommy handed her the basket with lunch, and he grabbed the blanket and jumped from the wagon. "Anna, where would you like the blanket?"

She smiled at him, then tapped her chin as if in deep thought. "Hmm, I am not sure, Tommy, where would you like the blanket?"

He turned in a circle, then headed toward a tall tree just a few feet from where they stood. The grass was tall and made the blanket lumpy.

Tommy looked around again as if trying to decide if he should move it to another spot. Anna saw the distress on the boy's face. She smiled inwardly and lay down on the edge of the blanket and rolled across it, flattening the tufts of grass. Tommy giggled, as did Mary. They stood next to the blanket and watched as Anna rolled back and forth. Once she stopped, she looked at both children and told them it was their turn to try because she was too dizzy to continue. She laughed out loud at the children's antics and realized how silly she must have looked doing the same thing they were currently doing.

A child's giggle caught Seth by surprise; he looked up from the baby to watch his new wife roll around on the ground. Then she said something to the children, and they jumped back up to their feet, and the children fell to the ground, starting to roll around in the same fashion that Anna had. Then the most magical sound filled his ears, Anna's laugh. Anna's face split into a beautiful full smile that had her eyes dancing. The children laughed like he had remembered, a sound he hadn't heard in far too long.

He walked to Anna's side and reached for her hand. At first, she flinched, then she relaxed when she looked into his eyes. He pulled her hand to his lips and kissed her knuckles. Then he mouthed a soft thank you. She only nodded and turned back to laugh at the children. He did as well, but not before he took a very ragged breath. Almost too soon for Seth's liking, Anna and the children settled down onto the now flat blanket. A few small pieces of bread, ham, cheese, and a cookie sat in front of each of them. Some cold water had been stored away in a few jars that had now been set in the middle of them all.

The children talked to Anna about the house and each of their rooms. They talked about the pony Tommy named Bo. Mary had a kitten named Freckles and one named Mitten. The milk cow was named Sally, and Pa's favorite horse was Dollar, but his second favorite was Whip. Anna fed Beth a bottle and then set the small child up in her lap so she could see the world around her.

Seth sat quietly through most of his lunch. The children's talkativeness surprised him, but he was enjoying every minute of it. He had missed this so much. They had grown so somber that it nearly drove him mad at times. He had dismissed himself from the house on more than one occasion to throw or hit something out in the barn away from the children's eyes and ears. He had begged God to help him; he had begged God to heal their sweet, tender hearts. He had seen small improvements in the months since Elizabeth's passing, but what was happening right now was what he had dreamed of. His heart swelled with appreciation for the stranger that sat next to him now, holding his sweet Beth and laughing with his other children.

For the second time that day, Seth couldn't think of one other man on earth who was as lucky as he was.

*****

The two-story white house that appeared among the trees took Anna's breath away. The large porch was wrapped around each side of the house, surrounded by rosebushes and what appeared to be lavender bushes. The barn stood to the side of the house, as well as a large chicken coop, and to the far left, a pig pen. A large vegetable garden set off to the right down a cobblestone path. Anna sat in amazement. Seth cleared his throat. "Welcome home, Anna, we all—" he said, motioning to himself and the children—"hope you feel at home here."

Anna pulled her eyes from the beauty all around her and looked toward Seth. "Seth, your home is beautiful," she said, almost breathless.

"Our home, Anna, our home." Seth smiled at her. "You are the lady of the house now, Anna. This is truthfully now more your home than it is mine, considering how much time I spend in the fields."

Anna smiled toward Seth, then pulled her eyes back to the house. This was now her home; she had better make the best of this. Anna waited for Seth to reach for Beth, then reached up for her. When her hand slipped into his, he squeezed it tight. Her eyes locked on him, searching the depths of the most beautiful brown eyes she had ever seen. He smiled and helped her safely to the ground, never taking his eyes away from Anna. She couldn't tell if he was trying to find something in her own eyes like she was searching his or if he was trying to gauge her reaction to the ranch. Either way, she was mesmerized.

She stepped closer to him. His one free arm slipped out of her hand to rest softly at her waist. She caught her breath, continued to gaze into his beautiful eyes. Then, as if breaking a spell, Beth reached for Anna. Anna jumped back and shook her head. What was she thinking? She reached out to Beth. "Come here, sweet girl. Your pa needs to help Mary get down. I better take you."

Seth watched Anna. He was absolutely taken with her. She was surprising him at every turn. She cuddled Beth to her chest and whispered to the baby. He smiled again, then shook his own head. He needed to get ahold of himself. He was not ready for a woman to be in his life, yet here he was, married again and enjoying himself quite a lot, actually. He reached for Mary. Once she was safely on the ground, he turned back to Anna. "Well, let's go have a look around, shall we?"

Anna nodded quickly, then turned back to the house.

"The main floor consists of the parlor, my office, the kitchen, dining room, pantry, and a guest bedroom. The second floor has four bedrooms, two on each side of the stairs."

Anna nodded again. "Makes sense," she added.

Seth held the front door open. She slipped inside and stopped in her tracks. The parlor was large and arranged nicely with lots of open floor space for the children to play. Two large chairs sat closest to the fireplace. The fireplace was beautiful, with a large river rock that reached all the way to the ceiling. A couch sat opposite the two large chairs, with a simple rug laid out in between them. Off to the left, she could see a desk and chair peeking out of a half-open door. "Your office?" She looked toward Seth.

"Yes, my office and my idea of a library. Books for you and me, as well as some for the kids as they grow."

She gave a quick nod in his direction, then walked further inside. The dining table was perfectly made to fit the space, with a total of eight chairs surrounding it. A small vase full of flowers sat in the middle, in need of fresh water. "Mary, why don't you replace these flowers? They didn't seem to enjoy being left behind, did they?"

"No, they didn't, Pa." Mary raced from the room with the sad-looking flowers in hand.

"Mary will replace the flowers each day, as long as we have blooms in the yard." He smiled Anna's way, then continued, "She has enjoyed flowers as long as I can remember. Even when she was just big enough to open the door, we would find her sitting with the flowers."

Anna smiled at the image Seth had just painted for her.

"The kitchen is just through here." Seth tipped his head.

She walked in front of him. The kitchen was spacious, with a worktable on each side of the stove and a much smaller table with four chairs and a high chair for Beth, sitting in the middle. As if sent straight from the Lord himself, Anna breathed a sigh of relief and headed straight to the high chair with Beth. Once she was secured in the chair, Anna rubbed her own arms. She wasn't used to holding a wee one all day. Her muscles ached in her arms. Turning around, she spotted a wooden spoon and snatched it up, then turned back to Beth. "Here you go, my sweet, play with this for just a moment."

Then she headed to the pantry. What she found inside were stocked shelves of canned goods. The floor held barrels of what she assumed was flour, sugar, and salt. She mentally told herself to check them all later. Then a washbasin sat next to the door. She walked toward the door and opened it. Peering out, she could see the henhouse, smokehouse, and root cellar. She nodded to herself; the house was set up well for the wilds of Montana.

Once back inside, she walked toward the guest bedroom. A nice bed with a light blue blanket stretched across it sat in the middle. A small four-drawer chest sat against the wall at the foot of the bed, a small writing desk and chair sat closest to the door. She nodded her approval again and stepped out.

"Let's show you the bedrooms upstairs," he said to Anna, then she turned as Mary and Tommy walked back in the door. "Watch Beth for a moment, please." Then he motioned for Anna to walk ahead of him. "Shall we?"

Anna gave a small smile and headed toward the stairs. Once she reached the top, she stopped. "Both Mary and Tommy's rooms are to the left if you would like to start there."

The first door she opened was definitely Mary's, a soft pink blanket covering the bed. White spindles reached up from each corner of the bed to about chest height. A chest of drawers sat against one wall, and opposite that sat a white desk and chair. The next room was definitely Tommy's; she laughed to herself if the green blanket that was haphazardly thrown onto the bed was any indication. The drawers in the chest sat a bit open, with the corners of clothing peeking out each one. The toy box full of building blocks had been tipped on its side, spilling its contents.

"It appears my cleaning lessons to the boy have not yet worked," Seth's voice broke into the quiet room.

Anna turned toward Seth and smiled. "Whatever do you mean, Seth? This room looks just like a little boy cleaned it." She giggled aloud to show Seth she was only teasing him.

Seth chuckled, "I must be mistaken then, for I thought a wild buffalo had broken into this room while we have been in town. Apparently it was only the wild son we have living here."

She giggled again. "Did you just compare that sweet, quiet boy to a wild buffalo?"

Seth chuckled again. "Afraid so, we better keep an eye on that one. Did you see what the child did to his toy box?" he said with a shake of his head, then added, "You would think he was raised in a barn."

Anna smiled and headed for the door. "I am sure he has spent a great deal of his time in a barn, so it is only natural for him to think such things, I am sure of it."

Seth followed Anna out of the boy's bedroom as she walked toward the other two doors on the opposite side of the house. One was the bedroom he slept in; one was the room Elizabeth had turned into her own years ago. Now a crib sat against the wall with a rocking chair and chest of drawers that doubled as a changing table for Beth. The situation at hand hit him like a mad bull cornered in a stall. Anna was now his wife but would she want to share his bed? Or would she want another bed set up in Beth's room? He hadn't put much thought into it. Well, in the last hour, maybe less come to think of it. Throughout the day, he had obviously thought about the fact that he was now a married man. He wasn't against marriage in name only, but they hadn't discussed the terms of their marriage.

Did Anna want her own space like Elizabeth had? She had wanted it because she had never and vowed to never love him. Therefore, she didn't deem it appropriate for them to share a bed. She had moved into her own room almost as quickly as the house was built. Anna didn't love him. She didn't even know him. So sharing a room with a stranger was problematic, to say the least.

She stopped at the door on the right, opened it, and stepped inside. His room? Their room? He didn't know. He froze in the hallway. Anna disappeared inside.

Anna took in the beautiful room before her. A large dark wood four-post bed stood in the middle of the room, a chair with a cushioned seat and back sat between two large windows. A large chest of drawers sat at the foot of the bed, with a tall matching wardrobe against the wall opposite the windows. A washbasin sat on a small wash table with clean white linens next to the door. A small desk sat at an angle in the corner with a small wooden chair. A dark blue blanket lay neatly across the bed. Anna ran her hand along the footboard of the bed as she crossed to the windows.

Seth entered the room at that moment; she felt him looking in her direction, but she continued toward the window and pulled back the white lace curtain to look outside. The barn and stalls took up the view to the north of the house, directly behind the house stood the smokehouse, root cellar, and henhouse. To the south appeared to be a good-sized orchard and a few rows of the vegetable garden could be seen. She turned to look at Seth. "The room is beautiful, Seth."

Then she walked out and turned toward the last door. A crib, rocking chair, and chest of drawers filled the smaller room nicely. The windows in each room brought in a good amount of light; they also helped warm each room, it seemed. The house was built with a lot of thought and love, she decided. "You—" She paused. "We have a beautiful home, Seth, I am sure you are very proud of it."

Seth nodded his head. "I am, thank you." Then he paused. He shoved his hands into his pockets. "I need to unload the wagon, umm, your belongings, where would you like me to put them?" His eyes looked everywhere but at her.

She smiled to herself. If he thought he was making it easier on her, he was mistaken. She felt so unsure of herself. She didn't know what to say. So she stood there staring at the floor. Seth shifted back and forth from one foot to the next. Finally, it looked like whatever war he was fighting in his head, he won. He looked up at her. "I don't want you to be uncomfortable here, Anna, this is to be your home." He hurried, "I would like you to be as close to the children as possible. Which would mean I would like you to stay in the big room. If you would rather I didn't, I can move into the room downstairs." He searched her face.

Anna knew she turned at least two shades of red under his gaze. "Seth, that is your room, you are comfortable in there, there is no need to move your belongings. I feel like we can manage in that room together. Don't you?" She clamped her mouth shut. She brought her hand up to cover her mouth. When had she grown so forward?

Seth watched the blush roll up her cheeks and down her neck. He grinned. She closed her eyes, took two long breaths, and opened them. "I am sorry, Seth, if that was too forward, I apologize. I just didn't want to make you move to an unfamiliar room. If the children came looking for you in the middle of the night, they would be mighty upset to find you gone."

Seth closed the distance between them and reached for her hands. "Anna, I want us to be a family. I want the best for this marriage. I hadn't wanted to remarry, yet here I am, in a situation I wasn't planning on. I don't want to start this marriage off on a bad foot."

He paused and searched her eyes for any signs of discomfort. "Seth, I don't mind sharing a room with you if you are not opposed to it."

Seth nodded his head and turned and walked out of the room. He hurried down the stairs and out the front door. He walked straight to the barn and slipped inside. He found the closest place to sit and plopped himself down, instantly placing his head in his hands and running his fingers through his hair. His world was spinning. Yes, he had thought about the fact that today was his wedding day, and he had once dreamed of a marriage full of love and tenderness like he had seen with so many couples. His parents had been a perfect example of what a marriage should look like. He had wanted that desperately with Elizabeth. But from the moment they had walked out of the church, he knew that was not what he was getting.

Thinking back on it now, he knew he hadn't done his fair share to make the marriage better, but a man can only take so much rejection before he just plays the cards in his hand. The cards that were dealt to him was a losing hand from the get-go. He had tried to change her mind, to change her heart. It had only left him angry and bitter toward the woman he had sworn to "love and cherish" in front of his family and God. He had failed them all. Now here he was again, married to a woman who didn't love him. She loved his children, which sent a shiver down his spine. Elizabeth had loved his children too.

He shook his head, stood up, and ran his hands through his hair one last time. He could do better than this. Anna was not Elizabeth; she was kind, not only toward the children but toward him as well. She had come from an awful marriage herself. He needed to make the best of this. She deserved better than the hand she was dealt as well. He had promised to "love and cherish" her as well in front of their friends and God. He had to at least try. He slipped back out of the barn and walked over to the wagon.

It appeared Tommy had already started unloading the items that he could carry. So Seth jumped in to take over the larger, heavier items. Grabbing a large box full of cans of food and bags of different baking needs, he headed back toward the house. Mary sat on the floor with Beth, playing with toys and singing a song. Tommy bounded past him on his way back out the door, and Anna stood in the kitchen, emptying a smaller box of goods.

"Got another for ya.'" She looked toward him and stepped back so he could place it next to the other one. "Change around anything you don't like. Make it your own, Anna."

Then he walked back the way he came. Tommy was jumping down from the wagon when he walked back out the door. "Thanks for the help, Tommy boy, I would be here till suppertime if I didn't have your help."

Tommy smiled up at his father. "You bet, Pa, I am happy to help." Then he headed back into the house with an armload of blankets the children had used to sit on.

Seth watched his son bound up the stairs with his arms full and smiled. The boy was growing up to be a fine young man. Although he would definitely need to talk to the boy again about keeping a clean room. The next armful of items Seth reached for was Anna's belongings. He paused before he reached out and grabbed the bags and lifted them easily from the wagon. Then he headed for the house. He took the stairs two at a time and hurried into his room. *Our room*, he thought to himself. He dropped them on the end of the bed, then ran his hands down his pant legs. He stared at the bags for a few long seconds before he turned and walked out of the room. He passed Anna on her way up the stairs. "I just dropped off your bags. I will finish up with the wagon and then I will be riding out to check on the men and cattle. I'll be back by supper." Then he took the last remaining stairs two at a time again and out the door.

*****

Suppertime was coming quickly. Seth really needed to be heading back home. However, after talking to his men, he found out a few fences had been torn down by the cattle on the north side of the back field. He wanted to check the fence himself before heading back home for the night, so Seth set off across the field. His mind wandered as well as his horse along the fence line. He noticed how well his hands had mended the fence in three different places and nodded his head in approval to the work they had done. "They did a mighty fine job, don't you think, Dollar?"

The horse moved his ears back and forth upon hearing his name. "What do you say, boy, how 'bout we run home? Anna's gonna tan my hide if I don't make it back in time to eat."

He turned the horse and gave him his head as he spurred the horse on. Dollar ripped through the field, enjoying the run as much as Seth. They rode into the barnyard just as Anna rang the dinner bell on the front porch. He tipped his hat and yelled from the barn as he jumped down off the horse. "I'll be just a moment, just need to take care of old Dollar here, and then I'll be right in."

Anna waved back and turned on her heel and disappeared through the door. Anna had always found a man on a horse to be attractive. What she didn't count on was being so darn attracted to the cowboy who just rode into the yard at a gallop, who tipped his hat and smiled at her. Goodness, that man had to know how handsome he was. She had almost stood there with her mouth flopped open, gaping at the man. Then she came to her senses, got her gaping mouth under control before she caught a fly in the darn thing, and turned her eyes away from the handsome cowboy. Goodness, she was a mess.

She hurried back inside with just a slight wave of her hand because she didn't trust her voice. It most likely would have come out in a high-pitched squeak, only further embarrassing her. She needed a minute to compose herself. She was in the kitchen, ladling stew from the pot when Seth walked in the back door, stopped and washed his hands, and removed his work boots. Then he appeared in the doorway of the pantry. He hung his hat on the peg and walked toward the table. "Smells good in here, Anna. Is that stew I smell? And fresh bread?" He wiggled his eyebrows at the two children who sat quietly in their chairs. They both giggled.

"I helped, Pa. I helped make the bread, and I cut up the carrots." Mary beamed at him.

"Well now, Mary, it smells like you did a fine job. Can't wait to taste it."

Anna placed the bowl of stew on the table, turned, and handed Beth the wooden spoon she had dropped to the floor and sat down. She turned to look at Seth and reached for Mary's hand. "Seth, we are ready for you to say grace, I suppose." Then she also reached for Beth's tiny hand.

Seth smiled and nodded his head. "All right, bow your heads, children."

Then he reached for Beth's other tiny hand and Tommy's while Tommy reached for Mary's. Sitting around the table with the family was a new experience for Anna. The simple chatter from Seth and the children all but took her breath away. It had been years since she had sat around a full table. Beth pounded on the high chair with the wooden spoon, and Anna turned to watch the baby. A smile spread across her face as she watched Beth play. Seth turned toward Anna and followed her eyes to the baby. He smiled at his baby, then at

Anna. "It won't be long, and she will demand to eat this stew right alongside us. I would be upset myself if I couldn't eat this good food."

He smiled again toward Anna. "This is the best meal we have had in quite some time, Anna, thank you."

Anna nodded her head. "You're welcome."

"It's real good, Anna," Tommy said through a large mouthful of bread.

Anna tried not to smile while Seth reminded Tommy not to talk with his mouth full. "I am glad you like it, Tommy, however, Mary is as much to thank as I am. She is the one who made the bread."

Mary's eyes filled with joy at the mention of her help in making supper.

Seth turned to his daughter and agreed wholeheartedly. "Mary, this bread is some of the best I have ever had."

Mary smiled at her father and beamed at Anna.

The rest of supper went smoothly. Everyone seemed to have enjoyed the first meal as a family. Anna was in awe of her new family. How her life had changed in the last twenty-four hours. Seth excused himself out to the barn right after supper to finish the evening chores. Tommy followed him out the door, and they both slipped into the barn. Mary helped with the dishes and took the slop bucket out to the pi pen. Anna decided that it was time to feed Beth. Once she had completed that, she planned to bathe both girls tonight; Tommy would be tomorrow, and then she would get on a weekly schedule with bath time. The smell of lavender floated through the house as Beth and Mary splashed in the warm water.

Anna laughed with the girls as she washed their hair and little arms. Once each girl had been dried off, redressed, and hair brushed, Seth and Tommy walked in the door. Seth paused at the door and yelled in from the washroom, "Everyone decent in there, ladies?"

Mary giggled at her Pa. "Yes, Pa. Me and Beth are squeaky-clean now, Anna says."

Seth chuckled back. "Well, now, how lucky am I? The two prettiest and cleanest girls in Montana live right here in my own home."

Anna smiled at the now full doorway as Seth stepped through the door into the kitchen. "Pa, there are three pretty girls in the house now, silly."

Seth looked from his daughter and back to Anna. "You are right, Mary girl. I have the three prettiest girls in Montana."

Anna's stomach fluttered under Seth's gaze. She tried to hold his gaze, but when it became too intense to continue, she turned her eyes back to Mary. The girl was dancing around the parlor; Beth sat snug in her arms, wrapped in a soft blanket. Anna reached up to run her fingers through the baby's soft, fluffy hair. Anna was trying to keep herself as busy as possible while Seth mingled around the house. He would shift his eyes to her here and there, and every time she met his gaze, her stomach would flip. Finally, she settled herself on the floor with Beth on her lap while Tommy and Mary played with different toys on the floor in front of her.

Beth squealed and flapped her arms up and down with excitement at her brother and sister. Anna talked to the kids and played with them all while laughing and talking about all the fun activities they planned for the next few days. Seth kept watching Anna; he was waiting for her to say something like Elizabeth would have. "Don't be so loud, you are playing too loud, don't be, ugh, so loud!"

Thankfully, he saw nothing like that. In fact, she was sometimes the loudest of the group while they played. He smiled to himself. Getting married was not part of his plans, but now that he had, he wasn't disappointed. So far, he was nothing but grateful for the woman who was now sitting on the floor, playing with the three people he loved the most in life. He would need to thank her later.

After a bit, Mary yawned and curled herself up next to Seth in his chair. Anna took that as a perfect excuse to start getting the children to bed. Soon she had a bottle for Beth; Mary and Tommy had made a trip to the outhouse, hugged and kissed their father, and were hustling up the stairs. She helped both Tommy and Mary into bed, helped them say their prayers, and tucked them each in. Beth was patiently awaiting her turn to be fed her bottle and rocked to sleep. "Okay, sweet girl, it's your turn. Let's go get you fed and rocked to sleep."

Anna slipped into Beth's room just as Seth walked up the stairs and headed toward Tommy's room. Anna assumed he would tuck each of the children in each night, which meant he would be in here shortly. She hurried to change the baby and settled into the rocking chair. Anna was humming a soft tune when the door to Beth's room softly opened. Seth slipped inside the next instant. Beth sat quietly in Anna's arms. She had just closed her eyes, so Anna placed a finger to her lips to keep him quiet. Seth nodded his understanding and then watched her closely and laid her head against the wooden chair. He studied her face. She looked exhausted, understandably so after her day. It had been an earlier than normal morning for her, he was sure of it. Then everything from the wedding to traveling, to making her first meal for the family, not to mention becoming a mother of three and a wife to a busy rancher. He mentally noted that he would need to help out a bit more for the next few days, maybe even weeks until she was more accustomed to her new life. Come to think of it now, as soon as Mary had shown any type of sleepiness, Anna jumped at the opportunity to get the children to bed. He hadn't really thought about how much her life had changed today.

He was ready to get back to work once they arrived home this afternoon. The few days of work had piled up on him since he left yesterday morning. His hands had always been his right hand when it came to running this ranch, but they hadn't known he wasn't coming home yesterday. They had made do but hadn't gotten to everything he had hoped they would have, so unfortunately, he had quite the workload today, which in turn had left Anna in the house alone with the children all afternoon and this evening. He hadn't meant to leave her all day, especially on their wedding day. But he had, and now looking at her, he could see just how wrong he had been in doing so. She was not used to this life; he needed to remember that.

Right now, he needed to get Beth into her crib and Anna into bed herself. He would pay closer attention tomorrow to how Anna was holding up. He stepped further into the room; Anna opened one eye to look in his direction. He offered a small smile and closed the rest of the distance between them. He stopped for a heartbeat before he bent and softly scooped Beth into his arms. The baby didn't stir, so he carefully stepped away from Anna and the tingle that scurried up his arms from his fingertips from brushing them across her soft hands. He pulled Beth into a soft, awkward hug and pressed his lips to her hair, whispered into her ear, and laid her down.

Anna shuffled her feet behind him, and he peered over his shoulder; Anna smiled a sleepy smile and walked quietly toward the door. Seth watched her go; he didn't know if he should follow or give her a few minutes to get changed into her nightclothes. So he stayed rooted to the spot next to the crib, watching his youngest child sleep peacefully. How many nights had he stood right here, watching his sweet children sleep? Standing watch over the cribs of his children had been a means of joy in his life. When Elizabeth had taken to sleeping with the children, Seth had had to stop looking in on his children because "it had made her uncomfortable" how his presence in a room had made her uncomfortable, he wasn't sure, but he had given in and allowed her, her space. He was beyond grateful when she had moved into the spare room, the room he was currently standing in. That had left him with the opportunity to once again take up watching his children sleep.

Now with Beth, he hadn't missed one day to check in on her. Elizabeth hadn't lived long enough to stop him from standing watch over Beth, and he had no plans to stop now. The joy each of his children gave him each day was something he couldn't measure. He was grateful for these moments alone with each of his children. He had wondered since Elizabeth's death if he would ever have more children. He was content with the three he had, but could he see himself as a father of more? He had been ready to welcome many children into his family years ago; Elizabeth had fixed that thought for him, though, again another thing he should be grateful for; at least she had allowed them to have a family. He was grateful to have any children at all, and he wasn't sure he wanted to press his luck with Anna.

Walking into a family with three children already, he could imagine was difficult; maybe one day they could talk about having children together. Maybe, but right now, he wasn't ready to think about that. Anna was different from Elizabeth. Even in the short time he had known Anna, he could already tell she would put nothing before the children. He was truly blessed to have married her. Then his thoughts shifted to Anna's late husband, Harold. He had been unkind to her; that didn't sit well with him. He was going to make sure she knew how cherished she was in this house. With that, Seth said a soft sweet prayer over his youngest child and walked quietly out of the room.

Seth stood at the cracked door to his and Anna's room. He wasn't sure if he should knock, then again, she had left it slightly open. Anna sat in the chair by the window, hands on her lap. She was in her sleeping gown, and her hair had been let down. Her eyes met his from across the room. Seth gave a slight smile. "May I come in?"

Anna nodded. "Of course, this is more your room than it is mine."

Then Anna shifted her eyes not quite to the floor, but almost. Seth smiled to himself. Anna looked scared to death. Seth had no intention of making her uncomfortable. "Anna, if you would rather I sleep in another room, I will. I want you to be comfortable here. Beth may need you in the middle of the night, so I think it is best for you to stay here. I will be comfortable with any bed after the day we have had."

Anna stood, took a long deep breath, then headed toward the bed. "And what side is yours?"

Seth again smiled to himself. She has a bit of grit to her after all. "I have always slept on the left side of the bed, but I would be happy to try out the right if you are accustomed to the left as well."

"Very well, I shall take the right."

Anna quickly made her way to the right side of the bed and pulled down the blankets. As soon as she had lain down, she pulled the blankets up to her chin and rolled to her side, away from Seth. Seth watched her, slightly amused by her actions. It had been a long time since he had shared a bed with a lady, and he wasn't sure what was deemed proper in this situation. This wasn't a marriage of love by any means; he was attracted to his new wife, but maybe it would be best for him to sleep in the extra bedroom. However, if Anna could be brave, then so could he.

Seth had sat down to remove his boots and socks. Then he stood and slipped off his shirt as well as his pants, then he pulled his nightshirt over his head. He walked quickly to the window and pulled it open just a few inches to let the cool breeze in. "Will having this window open a bit be okay?"

She answered with a nod; she didn't trust her voice. It wasn't long before Seth sat on the edge of the bed; she felt the dip in the mattress. She held her breath. Sharing a bed with a man hadn't worked out for her in her last marriage. She offered a silent prayer. She needed all the strength she could muster; she tried to calm her trembling body. Her fingers held tight to the blankets. She wasn't afraid of Seth; he had already proven to be a good man and a wonderful father. Yet her mind struggled to not imagine him using his hands the way Harold had used his. Then Harold would use his words to finish the job his hands had started. The sound of a man's low voice shook her to her core; now, after all these months of sleeping by herself, she once again found herself at the mercy of a man. This man didn't frighten her like Harold did, but Harold hadn't always treated her poorly. He started out kind.

She trembled again at the deceit that seemed to follow Harold around like a black cloud. She only wished she had seen it a lot sooner. Seth watched Anna struggle inside herself; he didn't want to cause her any stress. She looked absolutely frightened out of her mind. He stayed seated on the edge of the bed. "Anna, if you would rather I sleep elsewhere, please just tell me. I mean you no harm."

Anna's eyes popped open, and she took a long, deep breath before she dared speak. "Seth, this is and has always been your room. If anyone is leaving, it would be me. For I am the intruder here tonight."

Seth watched Anna for a few long seconds before he lay back onto his pillow. "Anna, this is now our room in our home. I don't know everything you have been through, but I know that my first marriage didn't fare too well by sleeping in different rooms. But"— he paused and waited for her to look his way out of curiosity—"I want you to feel safe, Anna. I would never hurt you. I would like nothing more than to share this room with you. However, only if you are comfortable doing so."

Anna stared into his beautiful eyes. They had been mulling this all night, it seemed. She needed to say something; she just wasn't sure what. She paused, bit her lip, but stayed focused on Seth's handsome face. She took a breath again and sat up in bed with her back against the headboard. He followed her movements, and soon they sat shoulder to shoulder. Neither of them said anything. This wasn't what she had expected her second wedding night to be like. She had figured that if she had ever gotten remarried, it would most definitely be for love and only love.

Today, she had married Seth out of necessity. Now here she sat next to what she believed to be a good man. Yet her body continued to tremble against her will. She stole a quick glance in his direction. He sat staring at the door, arms folded against his chest, pulling his nightshirt tight across his chest and arms. Goodness, the man was handsome. Then she mentally gave herself a stern talking-to. "Seth, we have discussed this arrangement a few times today. If you are uncomfortable with me being here, I can and will find another room to sleep in. Just say the word." She paused to gauge his anger. "I thought we had gotten on well together today. I am sorry for my own awkwardness and inability to hide my fear. I shall work harder."

She rubbed her hands together slowly. Seth had turned his head toward her, taken in her slumped shoulders, and how, with each breath, she seemed to shudder. "Anna, what are you afraid of? What happened that has made you feel this kind of fear?"

Anna snapped her eyes toward Seth's own. Tears stung her eyes, and it was becoming increasingly harder to breathe. Heat stole across her face, and a hundred emotions clouded her eyes. She was not ready for this discussion tonight. In all honesty, she hardly knew the man she was currently sitting in the same bed with. Telling him her deepest, darkest fears was not in her plans for the night. She quickly pulled the blankets from her lap, then stood at the side of the bed. "I am going to check on the children. You don't need to wait up. I'll be a bit."

Then she walked out the door. Seth knew it was forward for him to ask Anna something so personal so quickly, but the way he figured it, he had spent his last marriage fighting to talk to his wife. If she had been honest from the start, things would have worked out so differently. His life would be so different. He was not about to start another marriage like that. He had his own confessions to make, but something deep down in her was frightened; he wanted and needed to know what was troubling her so. He wanted to fix it, but he could not if she wouldn't talk about it. So here he sat on his wedding night, wondering if he would even see his new bride again before morning.

*****

When Seth woke up the next morning, Anna was not asleep next to him. He knew she wasn't, but he looked in that direction just to make sure. "Good job, Seth," he mumbled to himself, "less than twelve hours to run this wife off, new record."

Slipping from the bed, he dressed quickly and headed in the direction of the kitchen. The household appeared to still be asleep, so he decided against coffee until after he milked the cow and attended a few morning chores. The morning air was crisp. Seth stopped on the back step to take a deep breath and filled his lungs. Other than coffee, he figured the next best thing to wake a man in the morning was fresh air. He squinted into the early dawn light out across the fields. He headed toward the barn with quick steps. The sooner he was finished up in there, he could eat some of that bacon hanging in the smokehouse. Opening the door, Seth slipped inside and jumped straight into his morning chores.

From the front room window, Anna watched Seth slip into the barn. The kitchen stove stood cold, so he hadn't had his coffee yet this morning. He hadn't even demanded breakfast before he headed out for the day. Anna wasn't sure what to do with a man like Seth. Unfortunately, she found herself attracted to the man whom she now shared a last name with. She also found herself quite at ease when he was around. However, the not-so-distant memories of her last marriage continued to haunt her every move. Seth's low voice almost shook her to her core. He had never once been unkind to her, but that's how it started last time as well.

Last night, her body had trembled for at least an hour after she had slipped from Seth's room. She had paced the floor for another hour before the tears had overcome her, and she had settled herself on the couch. Sleeping on a couch when a bed sat but a few feet away in the guest room was foolish. Her back was already sore from the long ride on the wagon yesterday. Today, she would pay the price for her foolishness. When Seth had slipped quietly down the stairs this morning, Anna thought he had seen her. To her surprise, he walked past the couch without noticing her and out the back door.

Anna had stood and walked to the window to see which direction he had gone. Once he was inside the barn, she turned toward the kitchen to start a fire in the stove. She might not be ready to share a room with the man, but she would ensure he had a hearty breakfast before he headed to the fields. Anna was grateful for the full pantry to choose various items from. She had enjoyed cooking years earlier when she was able to. Now with all the needed ingredients at her fingertips, she could dive wholeheartedly back into her favorite pastime.

Soon the smell of biscuits, bacon, and eggs filled the house and seeped out the windows Anna had opened slightly. A soft hum followed the smells to Seth's nose, his ears picking up the sweet sound coming from the house. He stood just inside the cracked barn door and strained his ears to hear as much as he could. The hum would increase in sound, then switch to actual words from time to time. How long had it been since Seth had enjoyed the sweet sound of a woman's singing voice?

Filling his lungs full of air and his nose full of the smell of his breakfast, he headed back toward the house. The way he had figured it, maybe having a conversation with Anna this morning without the children within earshot would be best. The bucket of fresh milk sloshed at his side as he took the stairs at the back door two at a time. Better to get this over with quickly. He would start to sleep in the guest room. Anna needed to be closer to the children.

The back door opened, and a cool breeze followed Seth inside. "Good morning, Anna," he said with a smile. He would not allow their first night, or lack thereof, to keep him in a foul mood. He would approach each day with a gratefulness he hadn't shown Elizabeth. He had been in such a dark place with Elizabeth that even showing her how grateful he was for her, even if it was just for the children she had brought into this world, she had died without knowing that he would always be grateful for her. Her sacrifice to bring Beth into this world alone kept her securely tucked away in Seth's broken heart. Not broken because of the lack of love and kindness given to each other but for all that had been missed because of the opportunity missed. Seth knew he could have done better by Elizabeth, but his anger had set him ablaze; kind words burned on the tip of his tongue before he ever spoke them. Instead, he replaced them with hurtful words that still to this day made his stomach turn. He knew better; he had wanted better, yet he had failed. He had failed Elizabeth, the children, and himself. He would not make that same mistake twice. He needed to do better.

This marriage might not be one of love, at least not yet anyway, but he would be her friend; he would be a partner she could lean on and trust. He longed for the touch of a woman. A simple hand laid softly on a man's arm or the brush of her fingers against his neck while she straightened his necktie could make a man stand six feet tall. He missed the affection only a woman could provide. He would start this morning working toward just that.

"Good morning. I take it you slept well, considering your joyful mood," Anna gave him a sideways glance before returning her eyes to the bacon popping carelessly in the frying pan in front of her. She wouldn't admit that it stung just a bit, knowing he had slept so well without her. *Shame on me*, she thought to herself. *The man doesn't love you, Anna. He had lost his wife months ago. He has obviously come to enjoy sleeping by himself.*

Anna froze. Her mind stopped spinning when she felt Seth walk up behind her. The hair by her ears moved with his breath. A small, very small, and getting smaller step backward would press her back to his muscular chest. She closed her eyes, trying to focus on her breathing. She didn't want him to see or feel how unsteady she was currently feeling with him being so close. The pull to lean against him was strong—stronger than she had ever felt toward a man. She longed to feel the strength of his hands rubbing her sore shoulders from her foolish thoughts that sleeping on a couch after her day yesterday was a good idea. She wanted to feel his protectiveness surround her, pull her into the safety of his arms. The longing for all the good was overshadowed by the fear that ripped from limb to limb; her legs trembled, and her hands curled into fists. She couldn't take the pressure anymore; she turned to face him.

As soon as she did, she regretted it. Now she stood facing a very handsome man, who just so happened to also be her husband, staring directly into her soul. She felt herself getting swallowed up in that beautiful gaze, then his mouth moved, and she lowered her eyes to see one side of his mouth move, then the other into a grin that would send any female swooning. She pulled her gaze from his mouth just in time to realize her second mistake in just moments. When she had shifted her eyes to his mouth, his eyes had now found her lips. Joy, longing, and fear flooded her mind. When his eyes shifted back upward toward hers, he took that ever-so-small step toward her that now had them but a breath from each other. That pull she had steadied herself from earlier pulled again. This time much stronger, a strength she couldn't fight against.

She felt her body lean ever so slightly toward the pull; she closed her eyes. Seconds from feeling his lips on hers. Would it be a slight brush of his lips like it had been yesterday in front of the minister to seal their marriage? Or would it be more? And how long was he going to make her wait to find out? She could feel the rise and fall of his chest; she could hear his ragged breath. Could she sense those things in her as well? Would she have to plead with the man? Just about when she was ready to grab ahold of him herself, he closed the ever-so-slight distance between them, took a breath, and leaned toward her. She froze, waiting. Then Beth's soft cry filled her ears, and she opened her eyes at about the same time Seth took a step back. The heat and pull that had gathered in her stomach gave way to a cold uneasy feeling. He took a much-needed breath. "I'll grab her. You can continue with the bacon and eggs."

Anna didn't speak; she could only nod her head. She watched as Seth walked away and then disappeared up the stairs. Once he could no longer see her, she pulled her hands up to her face to cover the heat stealing its way up her cheeks. What had she done? Was she so lonely that she would all but throw herself at a man she hardly knew?

Then, smiling to herself, she thought a little bit harder on that very handsome man, and her cheeks reddened further. She couldn't explain her actions. Why she had allowed him to affect her like he had. She knew better, yet here she was, trying to make sense of a life she wasn't ready to accept. She trusted Seth, but not so much to throw herself at his feet and beg him to protect her. The bacon behind her popped and brought Anna back to her senses just as she heard little feet run across the floor above her and then trickle down the stairs. The bacon was overcooked, the eggs had formed a solid crust along the bottom, and the biscuits were a shade darker than they should have been.

Anna's face heated again, this time for an entirely different reason. How could she serve her new family such a horrible breakfast? Just then, Seth bounded down the stairs with Beth giggling in his arm. Mary and Tommy both greeted Anna with a "Good morning" as they sat down around the small table. Seth slipped Beth into her high chair and turned to help Anna pull dishes from the cupboard. His shoulder bumped into hers a few times, sending a wave of heat through her body as if lightning had struck her.

She closed her eyes for a split second before daring to look in his direction. That same handsome grin was plastered on his face. He must know what effect he has on her with that grin because he was using it to his advantage. She turned toward the table and set the plates with food in front of each child. Both Tommy and Mary stared at the mess of a breakfast they had been served. Both saying, "Thank you," they picked at their overcooked eggs.

Seth smiled. "Looks delicious. Thank you, Anna." He eagerly plucked a forkful of eggs off his plate and tossed them into his mouth. His heart was still racing in his own chest; he could only imagine how

Anna was feeling. She had overcooked the eggs, bacon, and biscuits, but who was he to be upset about that? After all, it was his fault. He would gladly take the blame for distracting his beautiful bride. His chest tightened at the thought of almost kissing her. He would be putting himself to task right now if he felt bad about doing it. He shamefully grinned at his plate. Then he reached for an almost black piece of bacon and pulled it to his lips. Right before popping it into his mouth, he glanced at Anna. She looked lost in her thoughts as she talked with the children or, as Seth noticed, the children informing her of their plans for the day. She nodded her head in the right places and offered one- to two-word replies when needed, but her head and heart were someplace else. She glanced his way just as he sank his teeth into the slice of crispy bacon. He grinned; she bit her bottom lip and turned her head toward Tommy. He was beginning to think getting married to a beautiful woman wasn't such a bad idea after all.

When the children scurried back up the stairs to get dressed, Seth lingered over his second cup of coffee. Anna stood at the sink, scrubbing the last of the breakfast dishes, while Beth played in her high chair with her new favorite toy, the wooden spoon. The pounding on the high chair seemed to go unnoticed by Anna as she hummed the same tune from earlier. Seth tried his best to ignore the pounding, but when he couldn't take it anymore, he slid out of his chair and headed to the sink to pour out the remainder of his coffee. Once he was next to Anna, his heart began to race again, and his chest tightened. "Thank you again for breakfast."

Without looking in his direction, Anna sighed. "It was burnt, all of it, but thank you for humoring me and eating it. Not sure the children would have if you hadn't. I'll make sure your lunch and dinner are better."

Seth watched the air rush from her lungs, taking her shoulders with it as they slumped. Seth watched her for a split second before she reached for his cup. *Do better, Seth*, he reminded himself. She pulled on the cup; he didn't let it go. She pulled again, and he grinned and still held tight, mentally begging her to look at him, pleading with her. If only she could read his mind. Then she slowly moved her eyes from the dish in his hand to the buttons on his shirt, next to the collar around his neck. She was getting there; he would wait forever if he had to. He leaned his head down slightly, figuring if she had come this far, the least he could do was meet her halfway.

Her eyes lingered on his grinning lips for half a second before she shifted her eyes to his. Time paused. The horrific noise Beth was making behind him faded; all he could see was her; all he could hear was her breathing and his heart pounding in his ears. "Anna, breakfast was perfect. I should be the one apologizing, not you. It was my fault the bacon was slightly crispy." He paused while he searched those beautiful eyes for the second time today.

"Thanks," is all she got out before he found himself pulling her forward. He couldn't quite figure out why he needed her in his arms at that moment, but he did. She stepped willingly into his embrace. Her hands braced on his chest, one of his hands slipped softly around her back, the other sat on her hip. He eased her closer and closer, enjoying the warmth she brought with her. She was like a flame, and he was a moth; he needed to get as close to that flame as he could. Once the gap between them was gone, he leaned toward her, then he paused.

Anna's mind was reeling; this was the second time in less than an hour that Seth had threatened to kiss her. She was already disappointed in herself for her actions earlier, and then breakfast was a disaster. Now he was inches from kissing her again, and he stopped. She wasn't sure why she was allowing this closeness with Seth; after all she had been through with her first marriage, she would have thought she was stronger than this. However, she had only felt safe with Harold for a few short days after the wedding before her ideas of a loving husband and children flew against the wall, shattering just like she had.

At Harold's hands, she had hit more walls, doors, tables, and chairs than she could count. Here she was, married for a brief twenty-four hours, and she had already let the walls she had worked so hard to build crumble at her feet. "Anna, I would very much like to kiss you."

Her breath caught, she licked her lips, she didn't answer as much as she just leaned closer to him, the gap but a heartbeat between them. He grinned, and she couldn't take it anymore. Clasping his shirt, she pulled him the rest of the way to her. Fire shot through her when their lips touched. This kiss was much different than the quick kiss they had shared in front of the Reverend yesterday. Yesterday's kiss was nothing; today's kiss was everything.

His lips gently brushed over hers, pulling her impossibly closer to him. The hand that rested on her hip now wrapped around the nape of her neck, pulling her even closer. His lips sought hers out again, this time not as slowly, but with the same gentleness as before. Then he stepped back, not letting go of her, but breaking the trance she was in. "If you wouldn't mind, I would like to kiss you every morning." He didn't wait for her reply. He smiled. "I'll see you at lunchtime."

It took Anna until lunchtime to calm her racing heart. Unfortunately for her, lunch also meant the return of Seth. Tommy had spent most of his day outside in the garden, playing in the dirt, digging for worms needed to catch fish. Mary and Beth had kept Anna busy most of the day, making cookies, bread, and lunch had never been so stressful and enjoyable. Mary jumped in to help with mixing, kneading, and setting the table. Beth made the background music, but other than that, she was a bit less helpful than Mary.

Peeking out the door occasionally to check on Tommy, Anna had kept herself busy, keeping her emotions in check. She wasn't sure what was happening with her iron-clad walls that seemed to disappear when in the company of a certain gentleman who just happened to be her husband; her stomach fluttered again. The back door opening with a whoosh of cool air, Anna set her hand on her stomach before she turned to meet the gaze of a very dirty little boy. Tommy gave her the same rakish grin his father had given her. She smiled. "Hello, you little ball of dirt, welcome to our home. I was hoping you could maybe tell me where a boy named Tommy has disappeared to?"

Mary giggled. "Anna, you are silly, that is Tommy!"

Anna looked from Mary to Tommy and back to Mary. "Are you sure, Mary? That does not look like the boy that went outside just a few hours ago."

Tommy giggled, then as did Mary. Seth took that opportunity to walk in the door, his children in a fit of giggles and his new wife standing in the middle of the kitchen with a look of bewilderment. "Pa, Anna doesn't think that's Tommy," Mary said, pointing at Tommy while giggling.

Seth looked over his son, taking in the gobs of mud and dirt clinging to his boots, clothes, hands, and face. "Well, it seems I better take this boy outside and wash him off. We might find Tommy under this mess. I am sure he would like some of that fine-smelling lunch."

Tommy shuffled his feet and headed back out the door, Seth hot on his heels. Anna figured she better grab a new shirt and pants for Tommy to change into. She hustled up the stairs and rummaged through the boy's clothes. Once satisfied, she hustled back down the stairs and out the back door.

Seth stood with Tommy over the bucket of water Seth must have gotten out of the rain barrel. "I have a few new things for Tommy to put on, once he cleans out his hair and washes that face and those hands," Anna said, motioning to the dirt that still caked to the boy.

"Thank you, Anna," Tommy said just before he plunged his face and hair into the bucket. With a slight giggle, Anna turned toward Seth, who had an "I am a proud pa" smile on his face. "Don't wait on us menfolk, my dear, we will be in shortly." The endearment sent Anna's emotions into a flutter again. She couldn't speak; she just turned tail and headed back toward the house.

Lunch was pleasant; the family talked and laughed together like Anna had always dreamed of. When she dared look in Seth's direction, he seemed to feel her eyes on him because as soon as she did, he turned his eyes from one of the children to hold her gaze for a few short moments before Anna couldn't take the intensity. Coward that she was, she would drop her head just enough to break the contact. Then she would focus on the baby.

When lunch finally finished up, Seth asked Mary to clean the table, Tommy to watch Beth, and then came to stand in front of Anna. Without a word, he reached for her hand and led her to the door, grabbing her bonnet and shawl, and ushered her out the door without a word. Soon he was pulling her down a small path through a patch of trees, winding away from the house toward what she thought she could hear was water splashing. Rounding the last crop of trees, the path opened into a patch of tall grass that sloped down to a beautiful river and waterfall. Anna's feet quit moving once the waterfall came into view, which in turn stopped Seth. He peered back over his shoulder at her with a questioning look. Then he followed her gaze toward the water. He smiled, then pulled her hand again to inch her closer to the water. She followed him without question.

Once at the edge of the water, Seth stepped closer to her. "I thought you might like this place. Whenever you feel like things are too hard, come down here and relax. Even for just a moment or two. I can't imagine how hard all of this must be on you."

Anna turned her gaze away from the water to search his eyes. He was giving her a place to relax. Even for just a moment? Harold wouldn't hear of such a thing. She was to be up thirty minutes before the sun and in bed no earlier than thirty minutes after the sun. She watched him closely, waiting for him to tell her it was a ruse and that she was never allowed down here again. But he didn't. He gave her that lopsided grin again. Her mind went blank, her knees trembled beneath her. The touch of his hand in hers sent warmth down to her toes. The butterflies in her stomach fluttered. She found herself locked into those deep, glorious eyes of his once again.

Then it happened again. Seth slid his one free hand around her waist, pulling her toward him by the small of her back. His hand that had been intertwined with hers came to his chest, pulling and urging her forward. Her breathing became ragged, her heartbeat at an abnormal pace. Pounding in her ears. The rushing water seemed to now stand still. "Anna," slipped from Seth's lips in a rush of air.

"Seth." Anna couldn't help the feelings taking over her body. This man was a good man, an honest man. He was so gentle with her that she practically melted into his arms. She closed the distance between them; however, this time he was going to have to come to her. It didn't take him long to figure that out, and so he got to within an inch of her lips with his. Pulling her ever closer, he waited for her to tell him no. When she didn't, he closed that distance and melted her to the spot. His kisses were sweet, soft, and full of need and want. She had never felt that with Harold. Harold's kiss was forced and unwanted. But she was too afraid to tell him no, so she endured it.

With Seth, she wanted and enjoyed them. She wrapped her free arm around his neck and buried her fingers into his hair. She felt wanted, not just for her kisses, but as a friend, wife, and mother for the first time in her entire life. Then he pulled himself out of her arms and jammed his hands into his pockets. Her heart sank. Here it was. The anger. Had she done something wrong? She felt cold, a shiver ran up her back. Knees that threatened to tremble right out from under her just moments ago locked in place. Her eyes dropped, taking her shoulders with them.

Seth cleared his throat. "Anna, I am so sorry. I keep taking these liberties without asking."

Her head snapped up. Her eyes danced with questions, needing answers.

"I know I told you that I would like to eventually be married in more than just name, but that eventually has come sooner than I had planned, I am afraid."

She continued to watch him, so he continued to speak.

"I feel a pull to you, Anna, that I haven't felt in quite some time"—if he was being completely honest, he wasn't sure he had ever—"but that gives me no right to push my affections on you. I ask for your forgiveness."

Anna stayed frozen. Even if she wanted to speak, she wasn't sure she could form a coherent word. She stayed rooted in place.

"I am sorry, Anna, truly sorry. I guess I hadn't known how lonely I had been until yesterday. But I will do better to control myself."

Something snapped Anna into action; she took three steps toward him, paused, then three more. He looked at her with worry and longing. Again, this undeniable pull anchored itself between them and inched her closer and closer. Seth's eyes grew darker and darker with each breath. That perfect grin crossed his face, and the sweetest side of Anna wanted to kiss that grin away. So she did. And she wasn't the least bit sorry for it. In just over twenty-four hours, every wall, every lock, every slap, hit, or push from Harold disappeared from her mind, and Seth filled every corner. His kindness and ability to make her feel safe warmed her soul.

She didn't know how long they stayed down by the river, but after being in his arms for whatever amount of time it was, it didn't seem like quite enough. "This must be what infatuation feels like," she thought to herself. As she held Seth's hand, they walked back toward the house. If sneaking away was the only way she was going to feel this happiness again, then she would plan an outing like this each day. With that, she smiled to herself. Seth caught the smile on her face; he smiled as well. She had to turn her head. She definitely couldn't go around kissing her husband all day. But she would like to.

*****

Over the next three weeks, the family fell into a smooth routine. Seth continued to kiss Anna good morning each morning but had moved all his belongings to the guest room after that first day home. The days grew warmer, work in the garden had begun. Tommy spent countless hours in the fields with his Pa, while Mary stuck closer to the house with Anna and Beth. Mary had become a perfect helper in the kitchen, while Anna took care of Beth and planned out the next meal of the day.

Baking cookies and bread had become a favorite chore of Mary's, and the child was quite good at it. Seth had not pulled Anna away from the kids since the day down by the river. To say she wasn't disappointed would be an understatement, but there was no tension between them other than that obnoxious pull she felt every time they locked eyes or she moved past him. Their arms would brush each other, and her heart would skitter to a stop, and her stomach would flop over itself. Even his morning kisses had become a quick greeting to start each day, not the earth-shattering kisses from three weeks ago. Today, Anna and Mary had decided to pack a picnic basket and meet the menfolk out in the fields for lunch.

"Mary, sweetheart, grab those cookies and stick them in this basket, please."

Mary reached for the cookies and skipped to the basket, stuffing them safely into an empty corner. "All ready to go, Ma."

Anna smiled at Mary. "Thank you for all the help today, Mary. I dare say this kitchen has never shined so bright."

Mary smiled sweetly and headed for the door. "Let's go, Miss Beth. It's time for us to get out into the sunshine."

Beth wiggled in her chair and slapped her arms down on the wooden high chair. Another smile split across Anna's face. This new life suited her just fine, she thought to herself as she pulled the baby up and placed a soft kiss on the child's soft cheek. "My, my, Miss Beth, it seems someone is finally growing a bit."

Beth squealed in delight at being picked up by the only ma she knew. The bond Anna and Beth had formed was precious.

"I smell lunch, but I don't see it."

Anna had been so caught up in Beth's beautiful smile she hadn't heard the back door open, and the two men in her life had walked into the house.

"Oh! Pa! You're early!" Dismay was plastered on Mary's beautiful face.

Seth turned toward Anna with a questioning look.

"We were just headed out to the fields to find you. We packed a picnic!" Anna said, reaching for the basket.

Seth smiled at Anna, then looked toward Mary. "Well, it looks like you ladies will have an escort to your favorite place to eat, Mary." Seth wiggled his eyebrows, and Mary raced back toward the door. Seth reached for the basket, then for the baby. "Tommy, will you grab that ole quilt for us, and we will be on our way?"

Seth ushered his family out the door and off the porch. Then he reached for Anna's soft hand. Tommy and Mary ran ahead of Seth and Anna, but to be honest, he was okay with that. He hadn't quite avoided being alone with Anna, but he had made the interaction quick. He couldn't really explain why, but he found himself in a strange place. Elizabeth had been pushed on him by her father; he didn't want that marriage any more than he wanted this one. The difference was he never had the feelings for Elizabeth that he was afraid had come naturally for Anna. He longed to be in the same room as Anna; her touch was nothing short of tipping the earth sideways. With Elizabeth, being in the same room was torture for a completely different reason. He enjoyed the torture Anna was putting him through; he dreaded Elizabeth's form.

Holding Anna in his arms all those weeks ago was nothing short of magical for him. The flips his stomach made just thinking about that day made the torture all the sweeter for him. The soft smell of Anna's soap hit him square in the nose; he inhaled all he could. Then he shifted his eyes toward her; she caught his movement and she turned toward him, and their eyes met. His feet became rocks; he could hardly move them. Anna's pace slowed as well. Beth pounded her chubby little arm on Seth's broad chest and squealed. Seth shifted his eyes her direction, then turned back just as quickly to search Anna's eyes. "Tommy," he yelled, "would you mind carrying this little lady for me?"

Tommy scampered back toward them without complaint and reached for his sister. Once she was safely tucked into Tommy's arms, Seth tightened his hold on Anna's hand, rooting her to the spot. Once Tommy, carrying Beth, and Mary rounded the first outcropping of trees, Seth turned toward Anna. He needed this woman more than he ever thought possible. The conversations, the glances, the mother to his children, their children he corrected himself, more of a mother than they had ever known. He smiled; she smiled; he took a step toward her, pulling her close. Once they stood only inches apart, he bent his head toward her. This time it was her turn to give him an innocent grin that made his head feel like it was full of cotton. All rational thoughts vanished. Then he kissed her. Not a simple good morning kiss like they had shared every day for the last few weeks, but a kiss meant for a husband to give his wife. One that he could only pray would let her know just how much she meant to him. The picnic basket forgotten in his hand, he dropped it to the ground to wrap his arms more snugly around her. Breathing her in had become quite a new and enjoyable hobby of these days.

The picnic went perfectly. The kids played at the edge of the water; Beth babbled to herself and rolled around on the quilt. Anna sat while Seth lay down and stretched out with his ankles crossed and his fingers locked behind his head; his wide-brimmed hat sat on his face, blocking the sun. A few soft snores slipped out from under that hat not long after he had lain down.

Anna smiled to herself. Looking around at her new family, she thanked the Lord for the hundredth time today, and it was only noon. While Seth slept the afternoon away, Anna sat with Beth, playing simple games with the baby. "Say Da-da-da. Come on, say da-da-da. I know you can do it. Come on, sweet girl, say da-da-da."

More baby chatter, then it happened. "Da-da-da-da."

Now it was Anna's time to squeal! "Whoo-hoo! Good job, baby girl! You did it," Anna said while clapping her hands in excitement. Seth stirred next to her, peeking his head out from under his hat. "Did I hear my baby say Da-da?" He rolled to his side. "Is that what I heard, little one? Da-da-da?"

Beth's toothless grin melted his heart. "Come here, little one."

He pulled the baby to him and rolled back onto his back, lifting her into the air above him. Beth giggled at him. Seth smiled that lopsided grin at his daughter; it seemed to have the same effect on every woman he gave it to because just when you didn't think Beth's sweet smile could grow any bigger, it did, and she giggled again. A small sigh slipped from Anna's lips. Seth shifted his eyes to Anna; the look she was giving him right now hardened his resolve to give this marriage more than he had hoped possible. He would move the sun and stars for Anna if that meant she would look at him like that as his reward. *Yep*, he thought to himself, *if that's what I need to do to earn the love from that beautiful woman, then so be it.*

Anna had never known a more involved and loving father than Seth; his children were the world to him. Maybe it was because he had been the only one around to care for them, or maybe Elizabeth hadn't been much of a mother. Either way, she was grateful for his attention to fatherhood. If she was being honest, having this handsome man as her husband had been the most appreciated blessing she had ever received from the Lord, so she sent up another prayer. Once she was done with her short little prayer, she looked back in the direction of her husband. He was still playing with his youngest child, making her giggle. He really was the most handsome man she had ever known. His heart made him even more handsome; she hadn't prepared herself for her newfound feelings for her new husband.

Then she sighed, his eyes shifted to hers, searching her face. She smiled. But that just made her heart race more. He shifted back toward the baby, then with a few more quiet words to Beth, he rolled to his side and placed Beth back on the quilt. Then he sat up and slid next to Anna, all while searching her face. She was trying to keep her emotions in check, but with him sitting so close to her, her emotions were front and center. "Thank you for lunch"—he paused—"sweetheart, it was delicious."

He watched her eyes widen with the endearment.

"This picnic was a fantastic idea as well. It's nice to spend a few hours relaxing with my family."

"I agree, it has been a wonderful afternoon. Unfortunately, I have too many chores to linger much longer." Anna sighed. "Some days, the work never ends."

"I completely understand." Then an idea popped into his mind. "The Tubbs family has a daughter. I believe she is fifteen or sixteen years old. We could hire her to help lighten your load." He paused. "She could move into the guest room, I could move into the bunkhouse with the hired hands, or even into Tommy's room. She could help with the children and the house chores." He studied Anna's eyes. "Only if you would like. She seems like a good girl. And I know the family could use the money. A flood last year drowned over half of their herd of cattle, and they lost the barn."

The inner war within Anna started when he offered to hire her help. She would love some help. However, did this mean she was lacking in some way? Had she let another husband down so quickly? She didn't know what to think. Then he said he would move out of the house; that made her insides tumble. She had hoped in time they would be able to get to a point where he would feel comfortable enough to move back into his room with her. Even though the fear that made her blood run cold chased away all the good they had shared, she still wanted him in the house. The bunkhouse was not an option. She felt protected with him close by; she couldn't imagine having to run across the barnyard to fetch him if one of the kids was sick or, heaven forbid, in the middle of the night. The thought of it made her insides shiver.

"Anna," he said, "I want you to be happy and comfortable." He continued, "I have my ranch hands to help me, maybe a housekeeper to help you would not only allow you a moment or two of peace but it would maybe give us a bit of time together as well."

He smiled a sheepish smile. Anna sat up a bit taller. "What is her name?"

"Emma," he answered.

"She can move into the guest room, but you," she paused, "you may not move outside. If I need you in the house, I will prefer not having to run through the dirt barefoot to come get you."

The thought of her barefoot running through the yard made the lopsided grin appear. She bit her bottom lip.

"So to Tommy's room I go. I can move in tonight. That way, we can get the room prepared for Emma in the next few days. It will be a day's ride over to the Tubbs' ranch to see if the girl would even want the job."

Anna nodded but didn't say much. Seth thought he could see disappointment cross her face; he wasn't quite sure why she was disappointed, but he didn't like feeling like he was responsible for it. In the next instant, she was on her feet, cleaning up the picnic and reaching for Beth. He got to his feet and reached for her hand just before she reached for Beth. "Anna, if you would rather us not hire her, we don't have to. I was only thinking of you. But if you would rather we didn't make the offer to the girl, we can think of something else."

Anna wanted to be angry, but how could she be? She would be more than grateful for some help, not because she couldn't do everything that was required of her but because she would like a bit of time to spend with the children that didn't involve work. She would like to start them on school lessons, and she would enjoy spending time with the handsome man with the lopsided grin that could turn a cloudy day into sunshine. Couldn't he see that the longer he stayed away from her, the easier it was going to be for them to live two separate lives as opposed to one family together? She wanted to grab him by the shoulders and give him a good solid shake. However, right now, she needed to get her emotions in check. She hadn't realized how much it hurt to have him pull away from her like he had the last few weeks. She had opened her soul to him, had trusted him. In return, he pulled away from her, keeping their conversations quick and without much substance to them. His kisses, though sweet, were not like the earth-shattering kisses they had shared right here in this same spot weeks ago. He was kind, he was gentle, and he was always willing to help her when she needed it. Why did he pull away emotionally then? Had she done something to make him put the distance between them?

Tears stung her eyes; she blinked quickly to try to push them back. She wiggled her fingers in Seth's hand, trying to get him to let it go. He only held tighter. Then, with his other hand, he lifted it to run his thumb under her eye to wipe away one stubborn tear that had managed to fall from her overflowing eyelids. He stepped close and wrapped her in a hug. His large muscles pulling against his shirt, her arms snaked around his middle, and she laid her head against his chest. Tears fell freely now, soaking her cheeks and Seth's shirt.

Anna hadn't allowed herself to cry that hard in years. She had taught herself to hide any and all emotion from Harold. Finding herself falling head over heels for three adorable children had been swift and completely unsuspecting. She couldn't help but love those three children. Then she found herself in the arms of their father, and time stood still; well, everything stood still but her tears. They fell freely down her cheeks at a rapid pace. She couldn't explain her emotions now. Everything she had held tightly behind walls made of stone now crumbled away in the arms of a man she wasn't ready to allow in. Yet, somehow, he had already pushed his way through those walls and landed right at her heart's door. All she had to do was open that door and let him in, but could she trust herself to do just that? Could she allow herself to love a man again? Had she ever loved a man before? Did she even know how to love a man? Or feel the love of a man in return? Whatever was on the other side of the door to her heart felt completely safe, warm, and giving. But she knew she couldn't unlock that door yet.

His hands made slow circles on her back, pulling her from her own thoughts and back to the sounds of the river, the laughter of the children, and the sound of Seth's heart beating against her ear. A steady thump filled her soul, steadying her emotions and tears. The slow circles on her back sent a wave of warmth through her body, her stomach flipping over itself.

*****

Two days later, Seth, Anna, and the children headed toward the Tubbs farm in search of a housekeeper. Sitting next to Anna for hours while they bumped their way down the road was again Seth's favorite kind of torture. Her shoulder would rub against his with every hole and rut in the road, giving Seth the slight touches he craved from his wife. He stole quick glances at Anna at every chance he got, trying not to get caught had taken up half of this trip alone. What he would do with his time on the way back was a whole new problem he would have to face shortly. For now, he could set his crazy thoughts aside, for the Tubbs farmhouse came into view as they rocked down the road. Tommy jumped from the moving wagon as soon as Jeb Tubbs spotted them. Soon the boys were bounding through the tall grass.

Edward was a giant of a man but kind as can be. The last year almost killed him when the flood killed half of his herd of cattle, then the barn was swept away. Edward and his wife, Rebecka, had narrowly missed being swept away as well, trying to save the family milk cow and horses, all while their six children watched in disbelief. Emma was the third oldest child at fifteen. She had two older brothers at eighteen and sixteen, then two sisters at fourteen and eleven, then Jeb who was nine. So hopefully, Mr. and Mrs. Tubbs would be willing to give up their oldest daughter for a few months, or maybe a year, while Anna got a little more comfortable in her daily chores and motherhood.

"Edward," Seth said in greeting. The men pumped each other's hands. "Hello, neighbor."

Edward nodded toward Anna.

Seth smiled. "Edward, this is my wife, Anna." He held his hand out to her to help her down off the wagon. "Anna, this is Edward Tubbs, our neighbor."

"Good afternoon, Mr. Tubbs. It's nice to meet a neighbor," Anna smiled.

Edward smiled. "My wife, Rebecka, is in the house. Head on in. She'll be pleased as punch to hear our ole friend Seth here has landed himself a mighty pretty young gal," he said, grabbing Seth's shoulder and shaking him a bit.

Anna smiled at the banter between neighbors. "I'll head that way then, gentlemen," Anna said with a nod of her head. She walked toward the house, shaking her head at the loud laughter coming from the men she just walked away from. Anna stopped at the door, knocking softly. The door pulled open in the next instant. A tiny little woman no bigger than a minute stood wiping her hands on her apron. "Good afternoon, Mrs. Tubbs. I am Anna Hillard. I am married to—"

She was cut off by a loud squeal that made her step back a bit before she was wrapped in a tight hug. "Seth has found himself a wife! And a pretty little thing too!"

Anna smiled. "Thank you, Mrs. Tubbs."

"Now, now, Anna did you say? You will call me Becca like most folks do around here. Now let me look at you."

She unwrapped her arms from around Anna and placed them on her shoulders. "Goodness me, my heart could explode with happiness. Our sweet Seth has needed a good woman by his side to help raise those youngins for far too long. Even when Elizabeth was alive, he had needed help. I don't like speaking ill of the dead, but Seth deserved better, and so did those youngins." Becca nodded her head at her comment. "Looks like he found himself the cream of the crop he did."

Anna smiled at her neighbor. "I am not too sure about all that, but I am trying."

Just then, Mary came through the door, holding Beth. "She woke up. Pa said to bring her to you." She paused, holding out the baby to Anna. "Pa and Mr. Tubbs are talking cows, ain't no place for a baby."

Anna smiled. "Thank you, Mary. I am sure she would agree."

Spending time with the neighbors proved to be a blessing. Anna learned so much about prairie life as a mother and homemaker. Becca showed her how to make the very best biscuits using lard. The wild berry jam they used to slather the warm biscuits was good enough to just eat out of the jar with a spoon. Anna was tempted. The menfolk had joined them on the porch after about an hour to continue their conversation in the shade. Another hour passed by quickly, and soon it would be time to leave. Seth reached for Anna's hand. She placed her soft fingers into his rough, calloused hand.

"Edward, Becca, Anna, and I would like to pay Miss Emma to come live with us." He paused, then nodded his head toward Anna; she smiled. He had to turn away from her before he lost all train of thought. "You see, Anna has not had a lot of opportunities in her life to raise children, housekeep, and make meals for a family. I would like to have Miss Emma come live with us, help Anna out with the house and kids when needed, make meals, and help with the schooling when needed."

Becca turned to her husband, then back toward Seth. So before she could say anything, he pushed forward, "I will pay a handsome wage, to both her and you, Mrs. Tubbs. I know without your oldest daughter here to help, the others will have to step in and pick up the slack. I will pay for that extra work. And, hopefully, it will only be for six months to a year. Every other weekend, I will loan her a horse and a chaperone home or bring her myself for a visit. She will also be home for any and all birthdays and holidays."

Anna turned her attention to Becca; she had turned back to her husband. "Can we have a moment to talk about this?" Becca said as she stood and headed toward the door. Edward followed close behind her. Once the door was closed, Anna let out a breath she didn't know she was holding.

Beth had fallen asleep in her arms, and her arms had started to ache. She shifted the baby from one arm to the other. Seth noticed her struggle and reached over to Anna, brushing his hands against her own. She caught her breath again, then her eyes flicked to his. He was watching her carefully. She found herself getting lost in his eyes. He smiled his perfect lopsided grin, and she melted. She smiled back, and warmth spread across her skin where his fingers still lin-gered against hers. All motions to take the baby had ceased. He was leaning toward her, his smiling eyes dipped to her lips, then moved back to her eyes, holding them rooted in place. His hand moved, the motion stealing the warmth it had given her. To her surprise, his hand landed softly on her cheek, her eyes flicked to his hand then back to his eyes, and she was lost in his stare. She didn't even feel herself closing the distance of their lips. He didn't hesitate to meet her halfway. His grin plastered on his lips disappeared as soon as he was close enough to feel her breath touch his face.

He looked deep into her eyes once more, waiting for her to pull away or say no—something. Elisabeth always had, so he naturally expected the same from Anna. When she didn't stop him, he closed the distance completely. Her lips felt soft and warm against his own, mesmerizing and perfect. She molded her lips to his. He reached with both hands to cup her beautiful face, pulling her slightly closer to him. He had kissed his wife multiple times, for that matter, but not one kiss had felt like this. This kiss was different. This kiss was a kiss that a man gave his wife when he wanted her to know and feel everything that he needed her to know and feel. He put everything into his kiss, hoping she would know just what was on his mind and in his heart. Then the door to the house squeaked open, and the moment between husband and wife was broken as they sprung apart like a child getting caught sneaking a cookie off the table.

Seth ran a hand over his face, then reached for the baby, not wanting to make eye contact with his neighbors as they walked back out onto the porch. Heat pooled in Anna's face, her neck reddened, and her ears burned. How embarrassed she was for being caught in such an intimate way with her husband. She hardly dared look at Becca. When she did, Becca had a slight smile on her face, looking like she was trying to hold back a laugh. Edward looked much the same. Anna wanted to crawl under a chair and hide.

*****

An hour later, the family, plus one, was headed back toward the homestead. Emma seemed excited and nervous all at the same time. Anna knew exactly how she felt. She had kissed Seth before, but this time, something felt different. She felt a closeness to Seth that hadn't been there before. Something warmed her all the way to her toes. The wagon ride home was full of nerves for Anna. She felt like Seth had pushed her away since the day they shared a picnic with the children. Today, it seemed he was grasping for her, and she was holding herself away from him. This felt different than anything she had ever felt for Harold. Her stomach would tie itself into knots just being around Seth.

His smile sent her heart skittering across the floor. His touch warmed her to the core. Her mind was playing games with her heart, and she wasn't sure how much more she could take. She was pulled from her thoughts when her shoulder bumped into Seth's. She turned to apologize only to find him smiling that troublemaking grin of his. All she could do was stare. He raised an eyebrow at her, his grin growing into a perfect smile. A bump in the road turned his attention back to the road. She continued to stare at the side of his face. How had this happened? She had been so strong, so unfeeling toward Harold for the last years of their marriage. She had been married to Seth for such a short time, and her feelings ran around inside her like she had left the gate open. She knew she hadn't done that; she had built the biggest and strongest walls around her heart. No way Seth had already knocked it down. So why did she stare at the man like this? She shook her head. She really needed to clear her head. She needed to get a hold of herself. She had been hurt too much to let another man in.

Seth quite enjoyed the look Anna gave him while they rode home side by side on the seat of the wagon. He smiled to himself once again. Anna was simply beautiful. She didn't need to dress up fancy or do her hair in some fancy updo to catch his attention. Unlike Elizabeth, Anna had a natural beauty that Seth found himself completely attracted to. Today, that kiss had been unexpected but much needed. He knew where he stood with Anna; she would never love him. But he had at least thought they could learn to care for each other. Becoming her friend was almost a necessity for him. Sure, he had his men and the children, but what he longed for was someone he could sit by the fire with at night or ride through the fields with on a warm summer evening. Maybe today was a step in the right direction.

The wagon came to a stop in front of the house. The children and Emma jumped from the wagon quickly, and Emma raced to Anna's side of the wagon and reached for a very sleepy Beth. "I'll take her, ma'am."

Anna handed down the baby. "Oh, please call me Anna. Ma'am makes me sound too old, Emma," she said with a smile at the girl.

"Yes, ma'am"—she paused—"Yes, Anna."

"Or," Seth said, coming around the wagon and holding his arms out to Anna to assist her down, "I have always liked the sound of Mrs. Hillard, even if I do say so myself."

That troublesome grin of his making another appearance.

"Yes, sir," Emma said as she walked away, cradling the baby.

Anna slid into Seth's waiting arms, her body melting at his touch. The air around her became almost too hard to breathe. She needed to keep her eyes lowered because she was afraid if she didn't, and he saw what she was hiding not only from him but from herself as well, he would think she was nothing but a foolish schoolgirl fawning over the new boy. She didn't want that, yet here she was again, wrapped in his strong arms. Soon, but not soon enough, her feet hit the dirt below them. She steadied herself and lowered her arms from his shoulders to smooth her dress when her eyes played a dirty trick on her and found his. Again, her heart skittered to a stop. She blinked and turned her head slightly to the side, breaking the contact. She took one step backward and forced herself to step around and past him. Once he was behind her, she took a breath. Her hands were shaking, and her heart was racing. The air around her felt heavy, her ears buzzing like a bee. She took another breath. *Calm down, Anna*, she said to herself. *There is no way he could have seen.*

She reached for Emma's carpet bag in the back of the wagon. "Let me, sweetheart. Why don't you head on in and show Emma to her room?" Seth said right behind her right shoulder, sending a shiver down her spine.

Seth watched Anna as she all but ran from the wagon and into the house. He ran his hand over his face and through his hair once he removed his hat. He wasn't sure what Anna was thinking or how she was feeling, but what he could tell was that Anna was uncomfortable in his arms. A part of him was okay with that. But a larger part of him needed to hold her more, closer, forever. He turned from the house and walked into the barn. He needed some time to work this out in his head.

Anna watched Seth slip into the barn through the window. Her heart wanted to be right there with him. Her mind knew better than to follow him. She needed some time to think. To figure out how she planned to hide her true feelings from him. She couldn't bring herself to admit just how much Seth meant to her in such a short time. She couldn't or, for better words, wouldn't let him break her heart like Harold had. She needed to protect herself. She needed to distance herself from Seth. She would make sure to have a plan by morning.

"Thank you, Mrs. Hillard. This room will be quite nice. In fact, I have never seen such a big bedroom."

Anna smiled at Emma. "Please, Emma, call me Anna. If you need anything else, more blankets, washcloths, anything, you let me know."

Anna turned to walk out the door. "Supper will be in about an hour or so if you would like to rest and wash up."

Supper was thrown together quickly; the children changed into their nightclothes and sent to the outhouse. Emma washed the dishes while Anna cleaned up the kitchen. They made small talk while they worked. Anna heard the terrible story about the flood, stories of her siblings. Once everything was cleaned up, they joined Seth and the children.

Beth had fallen asleep while playing on the floor. Mary sat next to Seth with her head on his shoulder. Tommy was playing with his horse. Emma stood off to the side while Anna went to Beth. Seth stood and reached around to grab Mary. "I think it's time to turn in, it's been a long day."

Tommy jumped to his feet and headed for the stairs. "Night, Emma. Night, Ma." Then he scrambled up to his room. Seth bid Emma good night as well and carried Mary to her room. Emma still stood off to the side of the room. Anna studied her for a few moments before she spoke.

"Emma, I really appreciate you being here to help me for the next few months. I hope you will soon feel at home and enjoy your time here, and please," she went on, "let me know if you need anything."

Emma nodded her head, then said, "Good night," and turned to go to her room. Anna watched the door close before she headed up the stairs to her family. Tommy was tucked into bed when Anna finally made it into his room after putting Beth down.

"Good night, my love," Anna said as she perched on the edge of Tommy's bed.

"Good night, Ma."

She ran a hand down the side of his face and smiled at him before standing. "Sleep well." She headed for the door, only to meet Seth at the threshold. He didn't move; she didn't move. She kept her eyes on the ground, refusing to look into his eyes for fear that if she did, he would read her thoughts. He would see her feelings for him and would mock her feelings, think her a foolish child. She would not let her heart break again.

"Good night, Seth," she mumbled in a quiet voice that barely made it to his ears. He stepped to the side, letting her pass him. He didn't say a word as he watched her slip into Mary's room. The last two days, he had done a fairly good job of avoiding her before bed. Sleeping in Tommy's room was comfortable enough, but it felt wrong. He knew that keeping his life separate from Anna's was one of the worst ideas he had ever had. This sleeping arrangement only put more distance in their marriage. He needed to fix it. Emma was bound to see his pallet bed on the floor of his son's room tomorrow when she went about cleaning. Would she tell her family of the real relationship between him and his wife? Would the kiss they had seen make them think badly of a man not even allowed to sleep in the same room as his wife, let alone a woman he had kissed quite thoroughly on their front porch? When he mentioned sleeping in Tommy's room, he hadn't really thought it through, obviously.

He stepped into Tommy's room just as Anna walked out of Mary's room. She turned her head in his direction, questioning his face, his eyes. He stood looking at her, unable to say anything. She squinted her eyes at him as if to study him, then she turned and walked down the hall, slipping into their bedroom and shutting the door. Seth changed into his nightshirt and lay on his pallet. Tommy's soft breathing let him know his son had already fallen asleep, so trying to be quiet, he rolled to his side, staring at the wall, wondering what Anna was thinking, how she felt, and if she was ready to allow him into a comfortable bed. If not, he thought to himself, he would bring a bed in from the bunkhouse.

He rolled his shoulder a bit to try to loosen the tension, then closed his eyes, willing sleep to come fast. He must have fallen asleep because the next thing he knew, he could hear soft footsteps in the hall. He rolled over toward the door, listening quietly. The steps got closer, then Tommy's door opened. A shadow stood in the doorway. Too big to be Mary.

"Seth?" That was Anna. He watched her walk into the room toward him. "Seth? Are you awake?"

His body felt like it was trembling when he sat up. "Anna? What's wrong?" His voice came out husky from sleep.

"Can you—" She paused. "Will you come with me for just a moment, please?"

He shook his head to clear it. He stood up from his bed and followed her out into the hall. He stopped once he closed Tommy's door but noticed she was still walking down the hall. He followed without saying a word. She paused briefly at the door to their room, then continued into the dark room. Seth couldn't decide if he was dreaming or if she was sleepwalking like Mary had a few years ago. But he followed her; she sat on the chair by the window. The moon shone in through the window, casting just enough light for him to see her hair hanging down in soft curls past her shoulders. The light gave her a halo-like glow.

He swallowed hard. Suddenly, he needed a glass of water.

"Seth, I am sorry if I woke you, but I needed to speak with you." She took a shaky breath. "I believe you should move back into this room." Her hands shook on her lap. Fear surged through her. "Emma will notice our sleeping arrangements, and I think it might give her the wrong idea." She paused again to take a breath, watching him, reading him. How had she known what he had only been thinking before he slipped off to sleep? He still didn't say anything; he honestly didn't trust his voice. So he turned and walked back out of the room, down the hall. He slipped into Tommy's room and started to gather his belongings. Folding the blankets and grabbing his clothes, he headed back down the hall, shut the door quietly behind himself, dropped his clothes off on the floor, and walked toward Anna.

She looked up at him with her beautiful eyes, tears pooling in them. He reached for her hands and pulled her to her feet. He walked her to the right side of the bed. Once she lay down, he pulled the blankets up around her and walked to his side of the bed. Anna felt as though she would tremble right out of the bed when Seth tucked her in; she watched him circle the bed. Once he was on his side of the bed, he pulled down the blanket. He sat on the edge of the bed, then pulled his legs up and tucked them under the sheet. Seth could feel the trembling coming from the opposite side of the bed. He took a breath, eased his own mind as much as he could, then rolled toward her. Without a word, Seth slid closer to Anna, slipped his arm across her middle, and pulled her to him.

Her back was pressed against his chest. She froze. Her mind went to all of the dark places she had tried so hard to forget. He pulled her closer, his breath on her neck. Fire shot through her body. He still didn't say anything, tucking her close to him. Her body seemed to know it was safe; it slowly molded to him, relaxing against his body. Sitting in the dark, Anna focused on her breathing: one breath in, one breath out, slow, steady, even breaths.

"Good night, Anna," Seth said against her ear, tickling her ear with his breath.

"Good night," she said after gathering her courage.

Soon, Seth's breathing evened out. She knew that he had fallen asleep. The rumble of his chest with each breath he took rumbled against her back. What she assumed would make her feel uneasy and frightened actually helped her relax enough to close her eyes. Soon her breathing matched her husband's. She drifted off to a peaceful sleep wrapped in Seth's strong arms.

*****

The sun was just starting to shine into the room when Seth's eyes opened slightly. He felt something shift next to him. Heat stole its way through his body. He turned his head slightly; Anna slept soundly next to him, tucked into his side, her face soft with sleep. Her lips parted slightly with each soft breath she took. He had to tear his eyes away from her lips before he did something he would regret. Instead of climbing out of bed as he normally would, he closed his eyes and pulled Anna closer to his side. She stirred slightly again, then settled back into a peaceful sleep.

*****

Her dreams were sweet and settling, as opposed to the nightmares she had experienced since she had married Harold years earlier. A slight snore made her jump, and her eyes widened. She looked right into the face of her husband. She studied his face, his beard hiding a lot of it, but what she could see made her heart flutter. She could feel the flush on her cheeks rise when he offered her a sleepy grin without even opening his eyes. He pulled her closer to his chest. "Don't get up yet there, sweetheart. I am going to enjoy this morning as much as possible, if you don't mind." His voice was low and husky.

She enjoyed the sound of it against her ear through his chest. "It's late, Seth. The children will be up soon." She chuckled when he pulled her even closer. The sound of her chuckle made him stick to his resolve of keeping her right where she was. The sound of Beth's cry made him groan. Anna chuckled again and tried to pull herself out of Seth's arms, only to be pulled back in tight, and then he moved to get up. Once he slipped on his trousers, he lumbered out of their room.

With Seth out of the room, Anna had a moment to herself to replay her actions last night. She had played out the look Emma would give her once she knew the truth of her marriage by seeing the pallet bed on the floor in Tommy's room. Would it be a look of sympathy like she had gotten after Harold had died? Or when members of the community had seen the bruises that he had left on her body? She had grown to hate sympathy. She couldn't bear to see that again. Now, because she had been a coward, she had invited Seth into their room to sleep. When she had offered it to him, she honestly didn't know what he would say to her. Turns out he wasn't going to say anything, and when he walked out of the room, leaving her sitting on the chair without a word spoken to her, she figured that was her answer. Then, after being gone for a short time, he walked back into the room, holding his clothes.

Her face heated as she remembered how warm his hands had been against her arms, middle, and the breath he had breathed on her neck as he held her close. Her mind was full of mixed thoughts. She wanted to bask in the joy of sleeping next to a man who seemed to truly cherish her; however, that ugly memory of Harold showed its face in her mind, and she couldn't get out of bed fast enough. She walked to the washbasin, splashing water on her face. The cool water was a welcome distraction from those memories that seemed to find her at every turn. Last night, when Seth held her so close, Harold's memory was gone. Now he was back, like he was back from the grave, letting her know what a worthless woman she had become, how lying in bed for so long this morning showed her weakness to live in this world, burning breakfast would cost her a black eye or two. She closed her eyes, willing him away. Last night, she had turned to a new chapter in her life; she wanted to enjoy not being afraid to sleep in her husband's arms, not fear them. But even from the grave, Harold was running her life.

After washing her face, pinning her hair up into a knot at the back of her head, she turned to grab her dress. At about that same time, Seth walked back into the room with Beth in his arms. "All cleaned up and ready for a bottle, Ma," he said in a childish voice, as if it was Beth speaking to her. Looking at the now empty bed, Seth scrunched his brows, then turned to see Anna standing like she was about to get dressed. He stopped. His eyes met hers. He held them, then sighed and walked Beth to the bed and laid her down in the middle, surrounding her with a pillow and blanket. "So much for taking it easy today, little lady. It looks like Ma is ready to start the day."

Beth smiled at her father and flapped her arms and kicked her legs while she made bubbles back at him. He chuckled, then turned to grab his shirt. Anna was rooted in place when he pulled his nightshirt off over his head. Then he walked to the water basin himself to wash up a bit before he started the day. Anna's mouth had instantly gone dry as each of Seth's muscles moved and flexed with each movement he made. Beth squealed, snapping Anna out of her trance. "Good morning, my love." She walked toward Beth on the bed. "You slept all night for your ma, didn't you, sweet girl?"

Beth continued to squeal, which caused Anna to smile at her. "Okay, little one," Seth said after turning from the water to dry his face, "let me get my shirt on, and we will head downstairs to get you a bottle."

Anna kept her eyes on Beth, fearing what he might see if he looked into her eyes. Anna picked the baby up and started to straighten the bed one-handed. When Seth walked to his side of the bed, she looked up when he started to help. Instantly, she regretted her decision to look. He hadn't finished buttoning his shirt; seeing him in this state of undress was making it awfully hard to focus on her chores, considering how flustered it made her. Once the bed and his shirt were tidied up, Seth held out his arms to Beth. She loved her pa, so she instantly reached for him as well. "Come on, you. Let's let Ma get dressed."

Anna handed over the baby, then again, against her better judgment, she looked into Seth's eyes. He was grinning that perfect grin, his hand reached out to hers, pulling her toward him with the baby. "Good morning, darling." Then he kissed her. She melted against him. Then he ended their kiss, and he took Beth out of the room, talking to her like she understood his plans for the day. Anna again found herself rooted in place until she heard the door click closed.

Seth placed Beth in the high chair and went about making breakfast. Emma slipped out of her room soon after. "Sorry for the late start this morning, Emma. Sleep didn't come easy last night, and I am afraid once I woke up, I didn't feel the need to get up right away." He smiled at her. "I am going to head to the barn to milk. Hopefully, the old cow will forgive me this morning. Will you keep an eye on Beth and breakfast? Anna should be down shortly."

"Yes, sir," Emma replied.

Seth nodded at her, grabbed his hat, and headed for the door. Once outside, he stopped and took a long breath of fresh air. Days were much warmer now, and he would enjoy the slight chill to the morning air before the sun's heat got to it. Once inside the barn, Seth headed straight to the milk cow. She was clearly irritated at his late arrival this morning. "Morning, Sally. Sorry I am late."

The cow whipped her tail in his direction. "Hey now," he said as he sat on the stool near her back end. "You can't blame a man for wanting to enjoy a little quiet time with his wife now, can you?"

Her tail flipped again; he chuckled.

"Morning, boss." Jake peeked over the stall. "Just about to head out, wondering where you've been." He smiled. "Now I seem to know." Jake put his hand up to stop Seth's reply. "I am not saying it like it's a bad thing, boss. I guess if I ever find myself a lady, I might feel the same way about my mornings as well." Then he turned to leave.

"Have the boys check the fences today and switch the grazing pasture if you can. I'll be out shortly!" Seth yelled to Jake's retreating form.

"Yes, sir!" was yelled in return.

Seth milked Sally, then headed back into the house with the bucket of milk. Once he got to the back door, he stopped; the smell of fresh bacon, potatoes, and eggs hit his nose. Today was going to be a good day, he thought as he opened the door, his eyes finding Anna. *Yes, a very good day indeed.*

Seth left the house shortly after breakfast. Anna watched him saddle Dollar and ride away. Then she took a deep breath; she was afraid that she had made the biggest mistake by letting him in. Now she didn't know what to do.

The day carried on as usual. Today, Anna planned to wash the sheets in Tommy's room, and the rest of the laundry in the house. Emma was asked to keep Beth and make lunch while Anna worked outside with Mary. Tommy was mucking stalls and taking care of the rest of the livestock around the farm, so Anna would keep an eye on him as well. Once she was in Tommy's room, she finished cleaning up the rest of the pallet bed Seth had been sleeping on and straightened the boys' room a bit before filling her arms with the laundry basket and heading out the door. She found a nice bit of shade close enough to the clothesline to easily hang the clothes once they were washed and got to work with Mary at her side. Teaching Mary how to wash was easy enough, and soon the young girl was begging for a chance to actually do the scrubbing on the washboard. Anna laughed a little inside, thinking to herself that it wouldn't be long before Mary detested the job as much as she did.

*****

The morning slipped away quickly out in the field. The men had the cattle moved and fences checked before Seth got himself out to meet them. Jake just smiled and tipped his hat at his boss while the others looked at him like he was a stranger. Seth was never the last one in the field, always the first. Today he was about an hour late, and the look on his hands' faces told him they wanted answers. Unfortunately for them, they were just going to have to live without any because he wasn't sure how to tell them that the first time he was welcome into his wife's bed after almost two months of being married was last night, and he wanted to enjoy the night just a bit longer than normal.

Seth tried to focus on his work; the problem was his focus was on a certain lady back at the house. Four or five cows snuck past him before Jake rode past him with a sly smile on his face. "It's all good, Boss. I'll grab 'em for ya. Maybe you should head back home."

Seth looked at Jake as he passed, then smiled himself. "I think you are right, Jake. I'll see ya in the morning." Then he spun his horse and raced across the pasture. Seth wasn't even sure what he was going to do. Maybe he just needed to be closer to her. So maybe he would keep himself busy in the barn or maybe he would start nailing down his plans for the addition to the house. The wood he had ordered should be delivered soon.

Seth rode into the yard at a gallop, tipping his hat at his wife and daughter. Both turned toward him. A smile and wave came from Mary; Anna fixed her bonnet, then raised her hand toward him. He had planned on heading straight to the barn but changed direction as soon as he saw the smile playing on Anna's lips. Slowing down, trying not to kick up any dust on the newly washed sheets, he stopped a bit away and jumped off his horse. "Afternoon, ladies!" He smiled as he walked toward them. He looked straight at Anna, eyes locked on hers. He removed his hat and slapped it against his leg, never looking away from her.

Anna stood rooted to the spot. Seth's eyes burned into her skin. He moved slowly toward her. She shifted her weight from one leg to the other. Her hands fidgeted at her sides; he still stalked toward her. Once he was standing but a breath from her, he reached for her. One hand went to her waist, one to her bonnet. Once his hand pulled her bonnet down, he used that same hand to pull her closer to him by placing his hand on the back of her neck. Once she settled against his chest, he lowered his lips to hers. He had never kissed her in front of the children, maybe a quick kiss before he headed out for the day. But not a kiss like this. Not a kiss that sent butterflies through her stomach and heat through her veins. He deepened the kiss before he stepped back.

Anna gasped for air; Seth smiled at her. "Decided I wanted to be closer to home today." Anna looked surprised, so he continued, "The hands have everything in control out there. Maybe we," he said, pointing to her and then himself, "should decide on how we want this addition to the house to look."

Anna's eyebrows came together. "You want my help?" she questioned. He smiled and nodded.

"The way I see it, this house is just as much yours as it is mine. Figure we should decide together."

Working with Harold had never been an option. So hearing Seth say that he wanted her input and help when it came to the house, she stood shocked for a moment. "Okay, if that's what you would like, I would love…love to help," Saying the word *love* stuck on her tongue just long enough for Seth to notice. She turned her face toward Mary, who had wandered toward the tree, trying to catch a grasshopper as it bounced in the grass. A rush of relief entered Anna, knowing the child had found something to distract her from the adults. Seth watched Anna turn her face from him, breaking the eye contact that had his mind spinning. Holding her in his arms last night, as innocent as it was to hold one's wife close, those feelings had kept him distracted all day. He had been worthless out in the pasture with his men; he had barely made it out of the house to milk the cow; now he was breathing the same air as his wife, kissing her silly.

That thought brought a small smile to his lips; he needed to be with her today. But just like she had yesterday when they had gotten home from picking up Emma, he watched Anna try to pull away from him. Maybe he shouldn't have taken the liberty to take her into his arms. Honestly, he hadn't even known what his plans had been when he saw her. It was like she was pulling him toward her without even knowing it. When she had allowed him to reach out and touch her, all he could think about was the warmth of her lips on his. There was no stopping him. Unless she had pulled away from him, of course, but she hadn't, so he had continued to pull her to himself and kiss her soundly. Now she was trying to avoid eye contact. Seth did the only thing he knew to do. He stepped back, then turned to head toward the house. He took the steps two at a time, opened the door, and yelled, "Emma? You in here?"

Anna watched him walk away, then heard him speaking to Emma; soon, he was headed back toward his horse. He mounted easily and walked the horse toward her. Emma scurried down the stairs with Beth in her arms and headed toward Mary and the wash-tubs. Mary reached for Beth, and Emma handed the baby over to her. Then she reached into the tub and started scrubbing the laundry. Anna turned from Emma to look toward Seth sitting astride his horse. She definitely shouldn't have done that; that grin of his was more than she could handle. "What is going on?"

Anna tried to steady her racing heart. Seth didn't say anything; he just moved his horse toward her and reached his hand toward her. Anna hesitated, looking into his eyes. Then she reached up and wrapped her hand around his. In one quick movement, he pulled her onto the saddle in front of him. She had used his boot to help boost her up; unfortunately for her, when she landed safely in his lap, she sat tall enough to look directly into his eyes.

"We'll be back later, don't hold supper." Then he reined Dollar around and headed back out of the yard at a trot.

Anna grabbed for anything to hold on to; the saddle horn was good enough for one hand, the other moved around Seth and settled on his back. Seth snaked one arm around Anna's middle while the other arm held onto the horse's reins at her back. Anna had to force herself to look away from him. Soon they had covered a large pasture, crossed a small creek, and wandered through a wooded corner of Seth's land without speaking a word to each other. "Whoa," Seth said quietly next to Anna's ear. His breath danced across her neck and cheek. She trembled under his touch as he steadied her with one hand as he slipped off the saddle and landed on the soft earth below them. When he reached for Anna, her heart skittered in her chest. She slipped slowly from the horse's back right into her husband's waiting arms. Her hands braced against his shoulders. The warmth of her body against his was almost more than he could handle. He could feel her tremble against him. He wished he could make her see that he could be trusted. Today, he hoped to do just that.

As soon as her feet hit the ground, he moved her over to sit on a log. The more he watched her, he noticed her eyes shifting around the wooded area, taking it all in. This was a special place for him. He had spent quite a bit of time in this cove among the trees when Elizabeth had gotten ill, then after she had died, leaving him with three kids to raise by himself, his heart ached for his children, but not for himself. Elizabeth had been a wonderful mother until she wasn't. He didn't mourn her for himself; he mourned for his children. However, he was no longer mourning for her.

His children smiled, laughed, and played like they hadn't lost a mother this last year. They played like they were genuinely happy, which made him happy beyond words. He aimed to tell her everything today, sitting in his special cove, under the canopy of the trees.

Anna watched Seth ground-tie his horse a bit away from them, then stiffly walk back toward her. He removed his hat with one hand. The other he used to run through his hair, then shoved his hat back on his head. He paced around the small area, removing his hat a few more times, shoving his hands deep into his pockets, removing them again, turning to face into the woods, then turning back to her. His features softened every time he looked in her direction but hardened every time he turned away from her. Whatever battle was raging in his mind, he seemed to only have trouble controlling it when he was looking elsewhere. She raised her eyebrows at him the next time he looked at her.

"Are you comfortable?" he asked her.

"Yes, I am fine. You, on the other hand, seem like something has set you on edge," she replied. He gave a small smile and nodded his head, then turned to pace again. She smiled to herself while she waited for him to gather his thoughts. Finally, after waiting for what seemed like a lifetime, he leaned against a tree facing her.

"I want to tell you everything, start to finish. Then if you would like to tell me"—he paused as if trying to control some underlying anger—"about Harold"—the name stuck in his throat—"but only if you would like to, of course."

Anna watched him before she gave him a slight nod to continue. He nodded in return, then started the tale of him and Elizabeth. Every detail burned into his memory spilled out in a story of great sorrow, anger with only highlighted bits of happiness with each birth of his children. Her entrapment of Seth into a loveless marriage just to get back at an old beau, the fact that she had used his kindness to keep him from turning her out to the wolves, even though she had deserved no less. She had loved the children, which he was grateful for. Then in time, she had also turned cold toward them. She never had the chance to love Beth, even if she had wanted to. She died so soon after the baby's birth that the opportunity had slipped from her fingers, even if she had wanted to grasp onto it with everything she had.

Anna shed some tears for the family that she now loved with her whole being, including Seth himself. She knew she had fallen hard and fast for Seth, but how could she not love the man? The kindness and love he had for the children would melt any decent and some not-so-decent ladies' hearts. His good looks only happened to make him all the sweeter of a prize worth fighting for. Unfortunately, she wasn't sure how to fight for a man who seemed too good to be true, a man who wanted to protect and comfort her. She had no practice with that kind of man in far too long. She knew it, but she didn't know how to overcome her fears. Instead of dealing with her fears, she sat perched on the edge of the stump, watching Seth. He didn't really look at her, more than for just a moment or two before his eyes would shift away to look through the trees.

When he admitted to not having mourned her life, that he didn't love her, that he was happy she had gone, he paused and watched her. He was waiting for her to tell him what a horrible man, father, and especially husband he had been to Elizabeth. But she didn't. She watched him, and then started speaking to him. She told him her story, a story she had wished she could dream away as the nightmare it was. Unfortunately for her, it had been real, and now she had to deal with the consequences of her actions. She told him about everything: the way Harold had treated her, she was his to do as he pleased, the lies, anger, drinking, and lack of food. With each word spoken, Anna watched flames come to life in Seth's eyes. His hands clenched into fists, then released before balling up again. When she finished her story, he stared at the ground.

What would he see in her now? Harold had told her so many times how colorless she was, how homely she had become. Her hair had lost its shine, her eyes grew dim. What would Seth see now? With her story out in the open, her burdens seemed to lighten a bit. She could feel some of the tension in her shoulders ease away. She still hadn't looked up at Seth; instead, she studied the little yellow flowers that had bloomed in the last few weeks of warmer weather. Seth pushed himself off the tree and strode toward her, stopping at the end of her boots. She still stayed looking down, so ashamed of herself. She had made the decision to marry Harold, sealing her fate. She had been ruined by a man who had promised to love her. She closed her eyes, trying to scare her tears back, when she felt a hand, then another, one on each of her knees. Her eyes opened to see Seth; he had kneeled in front of her, holding her in place, his hands sent heat into her bones.

He squeezed her knees softly, almost begging her to look at him again, to meet his eyes. She blinked again, and when she opened her eyes this time, she sought his. He studied her, tried to see the world through her eyes, tried to pull himself out of the depths of his own fear and anger to see her, to see the most beautiful woman he had ever seen, see her sorrow, her pain, her love, and kindness. His heart raced; his mind seemed clouded. But he had to say something to her.

"Anna"—his voice was husky—"I am so sorry, sorry for everything you went through. I am sorry if you believe that I have pushed my advances on you for my own pleasure as well. That was never my intention. I have never found myself dealing with whatever," he said, pointing to his midsection and heart, "this is, but I seem to not be able to help myself these days. For that, I am truly sorry." He stood and walked toward the horse. Was he going to leave now?

Anna shot to her feet, walked toward him a few steps, and then spun around at the tree Seth had leaned against. "Why are men so difficult to understand?" She thought she had said it low enough he wouldn't hear, but from the reply Seth gave her, it was obvious he had heard. She turned to him.

"I want to understand you, Seth, want to know you because," she all but yelled at him. She paused.

"Because what?" Seth asked. He had turned from the horse and crossed both arms over his chest. "Because what, Anna?"

What had she done? There was nothing for it now. He knew she was still hiding something from him. He could feel it. "Anna?"

She closed her eyes, took a long breath, and then looked him straight in the eye. She would regret this later, she was sure. But she would say it; she would reveal her last secret to him, even if it killed her to see his reaction. "Because you make me smile." He watched her with eyebrows pulled together. "Because you make me happy." He unfolded his arms, one shoved into his pocket, the other he used to lean on the horse. "Because I"—it stuck in her throat—"because I love you, Seth Hillard, because I love you," she rushed out. Her voice was so small this time she really wasn't sure he had heard what she said until she met his eyes again. He had definitely heard her.

With a whoosh of air escaping his lungs, he pushed off the horse and walked toward her. Her hands trembled at her sides; he pulled his hat off and dropped it, and in two steps, he had her pushed against a tree. One hand rested on her hip, the other right next to her head. "Anna," was the only word he got out before he covered her mouth with his own. His kiss was tender and sweet. She found herself reaching for him and pulling him closer, needing him closer. He obliged her by closing the small gap between them. After he had kissed her thoroughly, he pulled away just to rest his forehead on hers. Sparks flew through him. "I have loved you since the moment you raced out of the general store the day we first met. I didn't know I could love someone so much."

Her eyes opened wide, then she reached for the back of his neck and pulled him into another earth-shattering kiss.

She loved him, he loved her. She was kissing him, had pulled him to her. It was hard for him to wrap his head around it. She ran her fingers through his hair at the nape of his neck. And he lost all train of thought, and without another thought, he deepened the kiss. He didn't know how long he kissed his wife, honestly, he didn't care. When they both pulled away to catch their breath but stayed in each other's arms, he looked deep into her eyes. "Are you sure you love me?"

His grin, that grin that had caused her heart to flutter for weeks, now it made her knees weak. Good thing she still had her arms wrapped around his shoulders to keep her upright. "I am sure. I don't know how it happened, but it did."

Seth pressed his lips to hers one more time before he stepped back to allow her to slip away from the trunk of the tree. He walked toward the horse, checked his saddle, and then turned back to Anna. Her lips were still plump from his kisses. It made him smile. He didn't think she had ever looked so beautiful as she did right now. He had to shake his head before he pulled her back into his arms and spent the rest of the day kissing his wife. Instead, he offered her a leg up onto the horse's back, then he pulled himself up behind her. He wrapped his arms around her to grab the reins. It took all his will-power not to press a kiss into her hair, her temple, her cheek, right behind her ear. His list went on and on, but he had to stop himself. "Thank you for coming with me today. I enjoyed having you with me." He had enjoyed it. In fact, what was almost a wasted day had become one of his favorite days to date.

*****

After supper, the dishes cleaned, the baby fed, Anna walked Mary up to her room with Beth in her arms. Tommy sauntered up behind her. Emma turned in, and that left Seth sitting at his desk going through some books. Anna had watched him like a hawk all evening. He had noticed because he had done the same to her. He would grin, and her face would heat up, and then she would turn her head, breaking eye contact. Once all the shuffle of feet settled upstairs, he doused the lamp and headed up to tuck in the children. Tommy was already sleeping soundly; Mary chatted on and on about a new storybook Anna had told her about. He listened to her for quite some time before she finally yawned.

He kissed her cheek, pulled up her blankets, and slipped from the room. Beth lay sleeping in her crib as well, wrapped in a warm blanket. He ran his hand through her hair, bidding her good night, and headed to the door and slipped out quietly. Anna had already changed into her night rail; she was now sitting in front of the mir-ror brushing her hair, big curls flowed down her back. It looked like wheat blowing in the field. He had to touch it. Once he was close enough to reach out and grab it, he paused and then reached for the brush Anna held. She handed it over with questions rushing through her eyes. He stood behind his wife, brushing her hair, running his hands through it as he went. It smelled of soap and flowers. He pulled it up to his nose, inhaling its scent. Once he was done, Anna went to braid it. Seth stopped her. "Please leave it down, it's beautiful." He smiled at her in the mirror. "Almost as beautiful as you."

A blush ran up her neck and across her cheeks. He turned to open the window; when his back was turned, she stood and walked to the bed, slipping quietly under the blankets. Seth loved this woman, with his whole heart and then some. He wanted nothing more than to make her his in every way. It was going to take every ounce of will-power he had inside him to just snuggle up to her and hold her tight. But that is exactly what he did. Pulling her into his arms, he brushed a soft kiss to her cheek. "Good night, sweetheart." He felt her relax into his chest, making his heart soar.

"Good night."

*****

The months flew by as the family settled in with Emma; she had helped in so many ways around the house and with the children Anna never wanted her to leave. But it was time to take her home for a weekend visit with her family. Seth and Jake had decided to take her home first thing this morning. Once Emma was ready to go, the menfolk headed out to saddle the horses. Emma stood on the porch watching Seth and Jake work side by side. The children ran around the yard while Anna sat on the porch swing, rocking Beth in her arms. Anna watched Emma for a minute; the young girl's eyes were locked on the two men. Anna smiled to herself. How many times had Anna stood right there looking out over the yard at Seth the way Emma was watching them now? "I hope that look you have right now is for Jake, not Seth." She smiled when the girl jumped at her words. "Because if that look is for Seth, then we may have a problem."

Emma's face turned red as a blush crept up her face. "Oh," she stumbled over her words, "no, no, Mrs. Anna. It's—" She paused. "It's Jake." She paused again and turned back to the men across the yard. "It's Jake. I have grown to fancy him a bit, I think." Then her words hit her. "But Mr. Seth is a handsome man as well, he's just not Jake."

Anna laughed outright. "Emma, I am so sorry. I am only teasing. Jake is a very good man." She watched the young girl for a second more. "He would be a good catch."

Emma smiled at Anna and then turned back to watch Jake and Seth approach the porch, leading the three horses. Seth handed over the horses to Jake and bounded up the porch steps two at a time. Slipping past Emma, Seth moved quickly toward Anna. She stood just as Seth reached her, pulling her to him like his life depended on it, trying to be careful not to upset the baby in her arms. "I will be home by supper, darlin'. Save me a plate." Then he lowered his lips to meet hers, stealing her breath away.

"You better be," Anna replied as Seth bent his head to place a soft kiss on Beth's fuzzy head.

"Be good to your momma, little lady." He kissed the baby again, then placed another intense kiss on Anna's soft lips.

Once he broke the kiss and Anna had caught her breath for the second time, she whispered, "Go. Go, then hurry home."

He gave her that same grin that did strange things to her insides. Once Seth had helped Emma into her saddle and saddled himself, he tipped his hat toward Anna and rode from the house, turning back once before disappearing from view.

Anna had never spent a day alone at the ranch. Of course, the hands were out in the fields tending to the livestock and hay crop, but Seth was not here. He had always sent one or two of the hands with Emma for her weekend visits with her family; he had never gone himself. It unsettled her. The children played in the yard; Beth rolled around on a blanket on the floor near Anna while she took care of some mending. The windows had been opened to allow a soft breeze to enter the house, cooling off the early summer's heat that threatened to make the house unbearable. The summer kitchen had become a blessing as far as Anna was concerned. The soft breeze was now a simple blessing as well. Anna gave a quick prayer, oh how grateful she was.

The laughter outside the window grew still, the curtains made the only noise, the hair on Anna's neck stood, that uneasy feeling crept into her mind again. Standing to peer out the window, Anna could see Tommy running toward the house. Mary stood rooted in place. The look of pure fear on Tommy's face. Then, as if on cue, the smell of smoke filtered into Anna's nose. Panic set in; her eyes shifted from Tommy and Mary to just past the barn out into the fields. Black smoke billowed into the sky. Anna ran from the window and scooped up Beth. Tommy burst through the door the next second. *"Ma, fire!"*

"I see it, Tommy!" Anna was out the front door with Beth in her arms, Tommy hot on her heels. Mary snapped her head toward Anna when Anna yelled for her. Anna placed Beth in Mary's arms.

"Mary, take Beth, stay right here. Do you understand? I will come back for you." Then she ran. From where she stood, she couldn't see what direction the fire was actually moving. "Please be moving away from our home," she pleaded as she ran. Once she had a better view, her heart sank. The fire was headed right toward the homestead. "The barn animals, Tommy, you must let them go. They will be able to protect themselves. Go now."

Anna headed toward the pig pen and pried the gate open; this couldn't be happening, right? The henhouse was next as Anna ran to release them as well. The birds scattered at their newfound freedom; Anna just prayed they would be smart enough to get themselves to safety and fast. The smell of smoke had increased as the fire raced toward the farm. The smoke had started to settle around her, thickening the air and causing her to cough. Tommy burst through the barn doors, then ran toward Anna. "All of the animals are out, Ma. Now what do we do?"

Anna lifted her eyes to where Mary stood with a screaming Beth in her arms, tears running down both girls' eyes. Tommy was coughing hard, and Anna knew she had no choice but to run. "Tommy, grab your sisters and run to the picnic area by the river. I will be there shortly."

Then she bolted toward the house. She grabbed the blanket from the floor, filling it with food and a bottle for Beth. Anna could now hear the fire raging outside; it was much too close. Anna ran through the open front door and out across the yard into the outcropping of trees toward her children. Tommy stood with his sisters wrapped in his arms. Once they saw Anna, they sprang forward to rush to her side. Anna wrapped them in her arms, tears sprang to her eyes. "Children, we must keep moving and quickly."

Anna grabbed Beth, Tommy grabbed the bundle that Anna had grabbed from the house. Anna stepped into the knee-deep water and reached back for Mary's hand, pulling her into the water with a splash. "We must hurry, children."

The water splashed around them, soaking their dresses and Tommy's trousers. Without even thinking, Anna also allowed the water to soak Beth's clothes as well. Once on the other side of the river, Tommy scrambled up the riverbank first, then Mary. Anna handed Beth to Mary so she could lift her skirts enough to climb out. Once out, they ran.

Seth could smell the smoke long before he saw it. Once he reached a ridge and saw the smoke billowing up into the air, he panicked. Jake rode up next to him. "Boss?"

Without a word, Seth pushed his horse into a run. How had he been completely oblivious of the smoke until now? he thought to himself as he raced across the landscape. The trees had hidden the fire from view for far too long; precious time had been wasted. His heart was pounding in his chest; his lungs refused to take a full breath. Dollar's lungs protested under his saddle. "Come on, boy, don't quit on me now!"

The air around them became thick with smoke. He pulled his handkerchief up around his nose and mouth. The trail became difficult to make out; out of respect for his horse, he slowed him down to a trot. Jake rode up to his side. "Boss, how close to the homestead are we?"

Seth tried to look for landmarks that would be hard to miss, but the smoke was too thick; trees, rock ledges, anything that would help him determine how close he was to his home had melted into the smoke. The panic that raced through Seth took what little breath he had away; the homestead could be just a few hundred feet ahead, he just didn't know. How had his whole home disappeared from sight? He pushed Dollar into a run again. He had not been there to protect his family.

The barn was gone; his pigpen still burned; the henhouse, smokehouse, and home still stood. Fire had licked the side of the house, but his men had apparently made a wall around the side of the home, throwing water and fending off the flames with burlap sacks. His men looked spent, beads of sweat rolling down their brows. Jake jumped off his horse and ran to help his coworkers put out the last of the fire threatening the home. Seth ran to the open front door, yelling out for his family. Moving from one room to the next, yelling out. Nobody returned his calls.

"Men!" he yelled as he ran through the house, back out the front door. "My family! Have you seen my family?"

"No, boss. When we saw the smoke, we rode hard and fast to get to the big house to warn the missus, but when we got here, we couldn't find 'em anywhere," Elmer, the ranch foreman, answered.

Seth looked at the barn that had fallen in on itself. He looked around the yard; the fire had ripped through here, maybe twenty minutes ago. No animals in sight. Not even the noise of animals. He looked in the direction of the outcropping of trees that led the way to the river. "Elmer, are you and the other men okay to keep an eye on the house? I need to find my family."

Elmer nodded his head. "Yes, sir."

"Jake, you're with me." Seth jumped back on his already spent horse and headed down the burned-out trail, avoiding small patches of fire as he went. Once he reached the river, he stood in his saddle, looking around. The sun, which was already setting, was blocked by the smoke of the raging fire that was continuing its assault on the prairie surrounding him. He yelled out; he heard nothing in return. Seth crossed the river. Once on the other side, he looked to the ground. Were those footprints? "Anna!" he yelled again. Nothing.

The only noise he could hear was the crackling of the fire that remained in some of the sagebrush. "Anna!" He turned his head from side to side, pleading to catch a glimpse of his family.

"Boss, I think they passed through this way," Jake said, pointing to the ground at what looked like scuffled marks. Seth nodded his head and pointed Dollar in that direction. It couldn't have been that far, right? The fire had just passed through. They had to be close, right? He yelled and yelled until the smoke made his voice sound almost unnatural.

*****

Anna stumbled, trying to scale the rocky hillside. Tommy pulled on Mary's hand with his free hand. "Keep moving, children, don't look back, just keep moving."

Mary slowed to a stop. "Ma, my chest hurts too much to keep walking."

"Mary, sweetheart, I need you to keep moving. Tommy said the cave is not much further. We must keep going."

The fire had caught up to them once, scorching the hem of her dress even after soaking it in the water. She couldn't stop now. They needed to be safe. They had moved away from the fire; it still caught them. She wasn't sure what she should do at this point. She had no way to move any faster, yet the fire gained on them. She sent a prayer heavenward and pushed on. The rocks had been a godsend already. Rocks can't burn. The fire was now skirting around them for the most part. But the smoke and heat were becoming unbearable. Her lungs burned with each breath she took. She had placed a rag over both Tommy and Mary, and with her free hand, she covered Beth's mouth and nose, but that left her without a hand to cover her own.

Finally, after what felt like a lifetime, Tommy motioned to a cave just a few feet to her left. The relief that washed through her was not a moment too soon. She felt herself becoming faint; she made the final push into the cave that faced away from the fire, allowing her to breathe fresh, smoke-free air for the first time in way too long. She pushed her back against the wall and slid to the ground below her. Her head felt heavy; her lungs burned in a way she had never known. "Mary, take Beth, please," she said in a raspy voice. As soon as Mary's hands grabbed Beth, Anna gave into the darkness that she had been fighting so hard not to do. As the walls around her became nothing but never-ending blackness, she prayed that the children were now safe, then she was gone.

*****

Seth continued searching into the night, never stopping to rest. The fire had made its way around the next valley and moved across the open prairie to the south. A few spots continued to burn, but most of the fire had either moved on, burned itself out, or stuck around and smoldered in a sagebrush or two. The threat of the fire had passed. So where was his family? They had lost any trail of them once the sun had set. He needed to hear their voices in order to find them now. At the base of another mountain, Seth stood once again in his saddle, praying he could use the light of the moon to show him something. Anything. Nothing but blackness surrounded Jake and himself.

"The sun will be up shortly, Jake. Why don't you head on home, tell the men to spread out, look for the livestock, and get some rest?"

Jake watched the silhouette of Seth's form. "Boss, I would rather not leave you out here alone. I am sure Elmer will get the men moving first thing if he hasn't already. But if we find them, we will need both."

"*When! Not if, Jake! When we find them.*" Anger flew through his veins at the simple idea of not finding his family. "*When, Jake!*"

"Sir, it was just a poor choice of words. I apologize." Jake turned in his saddle to look at the sun's glow still tucked behind the mountains. "I'd say about an hour, boss, before the sun shines her light on us. Until then, which way do you want us to go?"

Seth pushed his anger aside. It wasn't Jake's fault. "I think we will keep heading this way. Daylight will come soon enough, I dare say." He pushed Dollar onward, settling into his saddle again. He rode on. Then he pulled Dollar up. "Jake, did you say something?"

"No, sir," Jake called from behind him.

Seth turned in his saddle once again, then stopped. This time Jake yelled out, "I heard it too, sir!"

Seth turned in his saddle, looking each direction, straining his eyes to see through the early morning darkness.

"Anna? Tommy? Mary?" He waited. Nothing. Dollar took a step forward then twitched his ears as if listening to something. Seth knew the horse could hear it too, but what was it? "Please, Lord, let it be them."

Dollar's ears twitched again. Seth studied his horse. "Where are they, boy? Can you hear them? You can, can't you?"

"Pa?"

Seth about fell off his saddle trying to see who had yelled to him.

"Tommy? Is that you, son?"

"*Pa?*" Tommy's voice broke. "Pa, can you hear me?"

"Keep talking, son. Keep talking. I will follow your voice."

"Pa, Pa, I am right here. You gotta hurry, Pa. It's Ma!"

Seth scaled the mountain behind his son as fast as he could, fear of what he would find once he got to the cave Tommy had told him they had hidden in. Soon he heard the soft hum of Mary's sweet voice, and he couldn't wait any longer; he rushed past Tommy and stepped into the cave, Jake hot on his tail.

"Pa!" Mary yelled, making the baby stir on a blanket next to her.

"Mary, my sweet girl. Are you well?"

Mary nodded her head, then her eyes shifted to an unmoving form on her other side. "Ma won't wake up. I have been singing to her, but she won't wake up."

Mary started humming a soft tune again, reaching for Anna's hand. The sun was nearly up, small specks of light filtered into the cave. Seth looked at Jake, motioning with his head. Jake understood. "Mary, grab Beth. Let's head back down to the horses and get you home safe and sound, how about?"

Mary hesitated, but after looking at her father and watching him nod his head for her to do as she was told, she stood, grabbing the baby as she did. As soon as the children walked out of the cave, Seth adjusted himself to get right next to Anna. "Anna, sweetheart?"

Her breathing was very slow, and her chest rattled with each breath she took. "Anna, my love, I need you to wake up." He rubbed a hand over her face. "Please, Anna, please wake up."

She stirred but did not open her eyes. Seth had no choice then but to pick up his lifeless wife and haul her to his horse. So he did. Holding her against his chest was exactly what he needed at that moment; he just wished she would wrap her arm around his neck to let him know she was okay.

The slow ride back to the farm was pure torture. He talked to Anna the whole time, but she never responded. Her eyes never opened. Her lifeless body sagged against him, demanding him to hold her up. He would. He would hold her for the rest of his days if he needed to. He just needed to know she was going to eventually be okay. He needed her to be. He could not lose her. He had been given a second chance at marriage and love; he needed her. He prayed whenever he wasn't trying to wake her up, begging God to let her live, willing her life over his own.

Once he arrived home, Elmer and Jake were at his side to help assist him in getting Anna off his horse safely. The muscles in his arms burned from the effort he had made to keep her held upright. Elmer headed to the house with Anna wrapped in his arms. Seth tried to protest, needing to be next to her, but for his safety and hers, it was best for Elmer to do the job. Once Anna was laid in bed, Seth turned to Jake. "The doctor? The children?"

"Doc has been sent for. Children are asleep," Jake said from the doorway. Seth turned back to Anna, still motionless on the bed. Her breathing, if anything, had gotten worse. "You get some rest, boss. We will be in with the doc as soon as he gets here."

Seth couldn't sleep. How could a man sleep knowing his wife was standing on death's door, if the blue around her lips told him anything? His heart broke in two just letting the idea pass through his mind. A tear rolled down his cheek. He brushed it away in anger. No, he wouldn't lose her. He would not lose her. He watched her breathing, willing her to take another breath, then another, and another. He slipped onto the bed next to her, watching her chest rattle, then shake and then relax. "Please wake up, my love. Please wake up." Then he drifted off to sleep next to her.

*****

"Seth, the doc's here," Elmer said from the door. Seth shot to his feet in the next instant.

"The children?" Seth asked.

"With Emma, a rider went to fetch her home. Figured you would need the help," Elmer said, and then stepped aside as the doctor made his way into the room. Seth rubbed his eyes, willing his mind to clear. How had he fallen asleep? What a horrible husband he had turned out to be after all. No wonder Elizabeth had never loved him. It was a wonder Anna did. Then again, maybe once she knew he had fallen asleep while she struggled to breathe, she would change her mind.

Seth shifted his eyes back to Anna. The blue around her lips was still there, the noise in her chest was louder, and her breathing had gotten worse. His heart broke in two again. What would he do without her? How would he manage life without—*No*, he schooled himself. She could pull through this. She had to. He wouldn't give her the option. He absolutely would not allow it.

"Children told Elmer she didn't cover her nose and mouth with a rag like she made them. She probably got too much smoke in her lungs, that's why she is breathing like she is," he continued his assessment of her, talking out loud but not directly to Seth, so he wasn't sure what he was even saying. Then the words, "Prepare yourself, Seth. It's up to her now. If she makes it through this, it will be because she has made a deal with the good Lord to let her live."

Seth never moved his eyes from his wife—his beautiful, wonderful wife. "I will stay through the night. If she makes it that long, then she may have a chance."

Then he slipped out of the room. Seth heard him leave but didn't see it; he couldn't stop looking at the one woman who had made his life worth living. He hit his knees and prayed, then with tears rolling down his cheeks, he crawled back into the bed next to her and held her hand, praying again and again.

A knock on the door startled Seth. "Sir, Doc would like me to change Anna into a night rail. Said it would be better for his doctorin'."

Seth nodded his head, kissed Anna on the forehead, and then slipped from the room.

Downstairs, he headed toward the voices of his children. Their somber voices reached his ears, a stabbing pain ripped through his already broken heart. How had this happened? Not a cloud was in the sky; the fire seemed to have just started on its own freewill, with no other plan than to rip him into two. It had done its job well. "Pa," Mary said, "has Ma woken up yet?"

Seth didn't trust his voice; he couldn't form the words, so he just shook his head no. Mary turned from her pa and walked toward the window. The house still had a strong smell of fire, so every window was propped open to allow for some fresh air to pass through. Even the front door stood ajar. "Can either of you tell me what happened?" his voice cracked. He closed his eyes to steady his emotions.

Tommy nodded and then started at the moment he saw the fire, finishing at him hearing Seth calling out for them. He told him how Anna had them wade through the water, soaking them up to their waists, and even dipping Beth into the water to soak her. He talked about Anna covering Beth's face with a rag but then not having a rag for herself. He told him about the fire catching them and burning the bottom of Anna's dress, even though only moments before, it had been soaking wet from the river. The heat was unbearable, the smoke was blinding, but somehow that amazing woman upstairs had managed to save his children from an agonizing fate. He owed her the world. After his conversation with his children ended, he had hugged and loved on them all; he made his way back up the stairs to be by Anna's side. He vowed to never leave again.

The dark of night settled around the house all too soon. The children's joyful laughs and giggles dissipated into the world beyond. And the tears Seth cried landed on a pillow next to his wife as he listened to her breathe. The rattling had grown stronger in the last hours. Her chest strained to take a full breath, but other than that, she hadn't moved.

*****

Anna made it through the night, much to the doctor's surprise. "Honestly, Seth, I didn't think she would have made it this long. The damage done to her lungs is something I cannot fix. She cannot breathe," he said, shaking his head. "I don't understand how she has held on this long."

"We can only hope our prayers are being heard." That was Emma from the doorway.

"I suppose." Still shaking his head, the doctor continued, "I would like to give her another once-over before I head back to town, then I'll be back out tomorrow afternoon."

Seth stepped away from the bed, then returned to place a soft kiss on Anna's forehead, whispering in her ear, "I'll be right back, sweetheart. Come back to me."

Then he walked swiftly to the door. He needed air. He needed Anna. He needed his life back. The wood that had been delivered a few months back was now being put to use rebuilding the barn; the addition to the home would wait. He made it to the front porch, then he headed to the outcropping of now-burned trees. How his home had been spared was as much of a miracle as his family had made it out as well. Once he was at the river, the smell of smoke heavy, he sat himself on a rock and cried aloud. His whole world was almost taken from him in the length of a breath. He could be burying his beautiful family today. His body shook with grief. He had prayed more in the last twenty-four hours than he could ever remember praying. And here he sat, finding himself begging God to grant him one more miracle, his Anna.

"Boss, you down here?" Elmer's voice rang through the air.

Seth wiped his eyes, trying to steady his voice before he answered. "Down this way, Elmer."

Just then, Elmer appeared on the trail. "Doc sent me to find ya 'fore he heads out. Said he would like to speak with you 'bout somethin'." Elmer stood with his hand pushed into his pockets, staring at the ground. Honestly, Seth appreciated the man more than he ever had at that moment. Knowing he had come upon Seth in a moment of grief, the man still gave Seth a moment to compose himself.

"I should be on my way then," Seth said, getting to his feet.

Seth reached Elmer's side, and Elmer cleared his throat. "Sir?"

Seth stopped. Elmer continued, "I am mighty glad to be your friend, sir. Me and the boys are grieving with you."

Seth put his hand on Elmer's shoulder, then watched a tear slip down his foreman's face.

"Me and the boys just wanted you to know you're a good man, Boss. We are proud to be here."

Seth watched Elmer for a split second, then patted him on the shoulder and nodded his head. "I appreciate that, Elmer, and I thank you." Then he broke into a jog to reach the house.

"Aww, there ya be, Hillard. I am just heading out. I'll be back tomorrow. I have given Emma a few things to watch for, and if"—he stopped and looked Seth directly in the eye—"if she wakes up, broth would be best for the next few days. Don't overdo it. But if," he said again, "she is to keep the baby growing, she will need something to eat." Then he stepped off the front porch. "By the look on your face right now, Hillard, I would say congratulations are in order." He tipped his hat, stepped into his buggy, and clicked at his horse.

The shock on Seth's face was evident. Emma stood with her hands covering her mouth, a new batch of tears rolling down her face. "Sir, congratulations are absolutely in order!"

Seth looked in her direction again, then nodded his head and bound up the stairs.

Once back to his chair by the side of the bed, he reached for Anna's hand. "A baby, Anna, we are to have a baby!" He reached over and placed his hand on Anna's middle. A little bump had begun to grow. How had he missed it? The first smile in over twenty-four hours spread on his face. Anna was giving him another child. His heart soared. "Please wake up, sweetheart, we have so much to celebrate. Please don't give up, keep fighting. Come back to me."

He kissed her softly, then sat back in his chair, holding her hand. He must have slipped off to sleep because he dreamed of a perfect little girl that looked just like her momma, beautiful curls bouncing around her face.

*****

Sometime in the middle of the night, Seth woke; he wasn't sure what had woken him, but whatever it was, it startled him. Then the noise came again, a deep, hurtful cough ripped through Anna's otherwise lifeless body. He jumped toward the bed, then another cough. "That's it, love, cough it out, keep coughing." Seth squeezed her fingers and ran his hand over her cheek. "Keep coughing. I know it hurts, but keep coughing."

Anna coughed a few more times, then settled again for the rest of the night. Seth climbed back into bed next to her, keeping her hand in one of his and his other resting on her middle. The darkness overtook him again.

*****

Early morning sunlight peeked through the curtains and landed on Seth's face. He stirred, then turned toward Anna; she slept peacefully. Her breathing wasn't loud. He bolted upright and reached for her fingers. They were warm to the touch. Seth sighed; relief flooded through him. Fears of losing her placed them in the forefront of his mind again. He needed to clear his head. He watched her sleep for a few more minutes, then he walked to the washbasin, splashing water on his face, praying he could make it one more day.

Anna felt the bed move, her fingers being grabbed with a touch of force, if she was being honest with herself. A small smile touched her lips; her throat felt raw, her mouth felt like she had been eating wool. A wave of nausea forced her to open her eyes, grateful to see Seth washing his face. Then he spoke, "Anna, my love, I need you to keep fighting."

He wasn't looking at her; his back was still facing her. So he hadn't seen her eyes fixed on his form. "I need you. I know you know that, but I think I will just keep telling you that over and over until you wake up."

Then he turned toward the window, propping it a little further open. He tucked his hands into his pockets and let out a long breath. "I cannot do this, Anna." His voice cracked on her name. "I have never loved anyone the way I love you. Losing you right now would break me."

Anna coughed. Seth flipped around to see her beautiful eyes peering up at him. He ran from the window to her side, reaching for a glass of water. "Anna!" he yelled; she flinched at his loud voice. "Oh, my love, I am so sorry, here, drink this water, just a little bit now."

He propped her head up a bit, and the water cooled her mouth and throat almost instantly. Then she motioned for more. Seth helped her again, then laid her head back down on the pillow.

The smell of smoke hit her again, and a flash of the fire stung her eyes; tears soon fell freely down her cheeks. "The," she tried to talk, but a cough ripped through her before she could finish. Once her coughing spell was over, Seth gave her another sip of water. "Children?" she said in a raspy voice. "Children."

Seth wiped the tears from her face with all the tending care he could. "You saved them, sweetheart. All three are happy and healthy. You saved them. Just like you saved me."

A small smile crossed her face, then her eyes grew heavy, and soon she had slipped back into a deep sleep.

*****

A while later, Emma knocked on his door, offering to sit with her for a bit so he could eat and stretch his legs. Before she could finish talking to him, he whispered, "She woke up, Emma. She woke up."

The look on Emma's face made him smile.

At noon, the doctor returned. When he was met with the news that she had awoken, shock wouldn't describe his face. "Well, I'll be," he smiled, "for such a little thing, she sure is a strong one."

Then he started checking her breathing, her heart rate, and eventually got her to open her eyes from her deep slumber. "Well, hello there, Mrs. Hillard. It's about time you woke up. You gave us all quite the scare, you did. Can you drink some water?"

Anna nodded.

After she had her fill of the water, the doc asked her a few more questions about pain; she tried to answer, but it just caused a fit of coughing. Eventually, the doctor ordered some broth to be brought to her. She eagerly sipped her soup, then relaxed back onto her pillow. Soon her eyes fluttered closed again, and she drifted off to sleep.

With a few more instructions from the doctor, he left again, saying he would be back in a few days to check on her progress. Then he was gone.

*****

The next few days were much of the same; Anna would wake up, eat and drink a bit, then she would slip off to sleep again. By the third day, Anna actually sat up in bed for about an hour before drifting off to sleep while sitting up. Seth, again, never left her side. The children had visited her multiple times; Mary had brought her wildflowers for a vase by the window. Tommy had drawn a picture or two for her, and sweet little Beth flapped her arms and giggled at her each time she saw her. The children had done a world of good for Anna's heart. They were safe, happy, and healthy. Seth stood quietly watching his family. His heart had never been so full. By the time the doctor returned on the fourth day, Anna was propped up in a rocking chair next to her bed. She had threatened Seth that if he didn't get her out of that bed, she would refuse to make him dinner once she was feeling better. He had laughed at her but had taken the threat seriously enough to help her move into the chair. The doctor checked her over again while she sat up. "Well," he said, "I think you are well on your way to recovery, Mrs. Hillard. Take it slow. Don't overdo it."

When she smiled, he continued, "Think of the baby, young lady." He replaced all of his instruments in his bag, then snapped it closed. "I'll be back in two weeks. If you need me sooner, just send for me."

Seth walked him to the door and thanked him again. A cough from up the stairs snapped his head in that direction. Then it subsided. She truly was getting better. Her voice had slowly returned to normal, her coughing was more sporadic; however, some of the coughing spells rattled her chest quite a bit. Today they had seemed better. Everything was better today.

*****

One month after the fire, the barn had been rebuilt. All of the livestock but two hens had been returned to their pens, and green grass had begun to grow off the front porch. Anna had started walking around the house at first, then she made it out to the porch swing, then to the new barn. Her lungs still burned when she asked too much of them, but she was getting stronger each day. She had also noticed the budding affection between Emma and Jake had blossomed into much more than just a few short weeks ago. She wondered how the Tubbs would feel about that. She smiled. Beth bounced on her lap, talking to Anna. "Oh really? And then what happened? Are you going to tell Momma?"

Beth squealed in delight.

"Oh, my sweet girl, how I love you!"

Mary and Tommy had spent hours out in the vegetable garden, removing the burned plants, replacing what they could, and pulling any unwanted weeds. Anna sat watching them now, another smile crossing her face. How had she become so lucky? Then a movement in her middle brought her attention back to Beth, then to her own stomach that had started to grow a bit more as of late. Another movement, almost like a butterfly rubbing its wings along her insides, then again. She smiled again.

By fall, Anna was back to as normal as a heavily pregnant woman could be. Each kick and hiccup felt almost unreal. Seth, if at all possible, had become even more attentive. Fall harvests had come and gone, the veggies they were able to grow, or regrow in the garden, had been put up for the winter. The hay had been brought in, and the fall calves had been sent to market. It had been just over a year since Elizabeth had passed away. So much had happened in such a short time. Seth, sticking around the farm more and more the last few weeks, had at one point said he would just go get the doctor and force him to live right here on the homestead with them until the baby was born. Anna knew they had at least a month, if not more, before the blessed event would take place, but Seth was not so sure. The doc had been out to visit two weeks ago, and she would be seeing him tomorrow when they made their trek into town one last time before the holiday season.

Anna was beyond excited to take the children shopping for a Christmas gift for their father. They had been planning for weeks. The joy of being able to shop at any given time was not lost on her; what a blessing this last year had been for her. Three, almost four beautiful children to love, and the love of a good man had been handed to her by no one other than God Himself, and she tried to thank Him every chance she got.

*****

The days had grown shorter. The evenings had become colder; the weather was changing, and soon their family would be changing too. Christmas was a joyous time at the Hillard ranch. A beautiful tree adorned the corner of the sitting room. Popcorn had been strung amongst its branches. Gifts sat wrapped beneath it, driving the children crazy with anticipation. Anna hadn't remembered the joy of Christmas living with Harold. A few of the year's Christmases had come and gone, and she hadn't even known. Of course, she knew the day was soon or just past. But the actual day was not celebrated. And never had she been able to buy or receive one gift, let alone for a whole family. The Christmas feast she had created included a large turkey Seth had gotten while hunting a few days earlier.

Potatoes, winter squash from the garden, rolls, and fruit preserves. A pumpkin pie and cinnamon buns made the house smell like heaven. Here she sat at the table with her family, holding hands and praying over the wonderful meal, a baby kicking in her belly. Anna finally felt secure, happy, and content. What a wonderful gift God had given her.

On the morning of January tenth, Anna felt a sharp pain in her back. Sitting upright in bed with one hand on her belly and one hand on the bed to help her balance, gasping for breath. Seth rolled to his side, then, as if the strange noise to his side finally registered in his sleep-ridden mind, sat up as well.

"Anna, are you—" He stopped, watching her take another breath, pushing slightly on her middle. "Is it time?" he asked.

Anna could only nod; the pains were coming close together; she focused on catching her breath, not talking. Seth piled out of bed, dressed quickly, and ran down the stairs to Emma.

Emma, being the third oldest child of her family, had helped her own mother give birth multiple times. He reached her door, knocking. "Emma, Emma, it's Anna, it's the baby." He waited just a few seconds, then knocked again. "Emma?"

At that moment, the door opened, and Emma stepped past him and headed up the stairs. "Rags, warm water, and fresh water for her washbasin." Then she disappeared up the stairs.

Seth did as he was told. He didn't need to be asked twice. Within minutes, he was walking through the door with clean rags and some water to replace what was already in the washbasin. "Warm water will be only a few short minutes. What else can I do?"

Emma smiled briefly at him, then another pain ripped through Anna, and she returned her attention back to her patient. "Nothing at the moment, Mr. Hillard. Just bring the water when it's ready and keep it coming throughout the day. We will want it on hand for the new babe."

Seth looked at Anna, the pain evident on her face, beads of sweat forming on her forehead. Emma wiped at them with a cool cloth. He nodded his head. "I'll be just outside the door, if you need me."

Anna smiled at him briefly, then gripped the sheets with her fingers as pain seared through her.

Hours passed, and the only sound that he could hear was Emma's calm voice and occasional noises from Anna herself. Then someone would move, feet would cross the floor, stop, and then return again to where they had come from. Each time Seth refreshed the water, he would steal a peek at his beautiful wife struggling to bring their child into the world. He would ask again if there was anything else he could do; he was always told the same thing, "No, sir," then pushed out the door. The other children stuck close to his side all day, into the evening, and soon after the night as they waited for any news of a new brother or sister.

A cry sounded, faint but definitely a cry. Seth jumped to his feet and headed for the stairs. Movement on the door above his head caught his attention, then another cry. He knew the baby was finally here. He bolted up the stairs, just reaching for the door handle when it opened, and Emma stood in front of him.

The pain of childbirth was not something Anna would soon forget. Emma had helped her through it all. "One more big push, Anna, and you will get to meet your baby."

Anna took a deep breath and did as she was told, and to her surprise, it actually worked. Emma placed a tiny baby on her chest. "It looks like Tommy boy got his wish," Emma said. "It's a boy."

Tears raced down Anna's face as she stared into the eyes of her baby; she couldn't believe it. Her baby. Then another pain burned through her insides. She needed to push. "Emma, something is—" The pain became too much, and she quit talking. "Anna, I need you to breathe and give me that baby."

The pain was so intense that despite wanting to continue to hold her son, she knew it wasn't safe. Emma placed the baby in a basket by the bed; his tiny cries broke her heart, yet she could do nothing to hold him at the moment. "Anna, push, I need you to push." Again, Anna did as she was told, then stopped to catch her breath. "No, Anna, push, keep pushing."

Then with one more push, Emma placed another tiny baby on her chest. "It appears Mary got her wish as well. It's a girl."

Two tiny cries floated to Anna's ears; her need to hold them both overwhelmed her beyond measure. As soon as Emma got both babies and Anna cleaned up, she walked to the door. Once she opened it, she came face-to-face with the man she was looking for. "Oh, sir, you frightened me." She stepped to the side to let him in the room. "Congratulations to you both. I'll leave you for a moment, check in on the others."

Seth's eyes settled on his wife as soon as that door opened; there she sat, holding one baby in her left arm and one in her right. Anna smiled a sleepy smile. "Would you like to meet your son?" she said, holding up her right arm. "And your daughter?" she said, holding up her left.

A small cry filled the room; Seth couldn't stop the smile or the tears that stung his eyes. "We have twins?" He laughed aloud. "Twins?"

Anna nodded her head. "Now we need two names." She giggled slightly. "They are beautiful."

She looked into his eyes. "Are you going to stand over there for the rest of the night, Mr. Hillard?" she asked. All of a sudden, the shock set in, and he was swiftly at her side. He reached for his daughter first, then his new son, holding them both as close to his chest as he could. They seemed so tiny in his big hands. His smile spread across his face. "How on earth did we not know?" He laughed again. "I cannot believe we have twins."

Anna's tears had begun to fall freely again, and she rested her head back just a bit; she was becoming increasingly tired, afraid she would fall asleep sitting up. "Well, what should we call them?" she asked.

He just stood at her side, shaking his head. "I am not sure." He couldn't get over their perfect little faces and tiny little fingers poking out from beneath their blankets.

"Lilly and Oliver?" she asked. He looked back down at his precious new children. "What do you two think? Do you like Lilly and Oliver?"

Both babies slept soundly in his arms. "I believe you have just given me not only two perfect children, but you gave them two perfect names as well."

Anna smiled at her husband holding the babies. Then she drifted off to sleep.

*****

The cry of a baby, then the voice of her husband filled Anna's ears. Her eyes were heavy, but she forced them open. "Anna, sweetheart, Oliver seems to be quite hungry. And I am sure Lilly will soon be as well," he said with a smile.

"Oh, of course, I am so sorry, sweet boy, Momma must have drifted off to sleep."

She shifted until she was in a sitting position, then reached for her son. Holding him in her hands, she held him up to her nose, rubbing his against her own. "Are you hungry, little man?" She smiled at him, then turned her eyes toward Seth. "Go ahead and leave her right here next to me. I'll get them fed."

"Okay, my little Lilly, you are going to stay here with your momma and big brother," he said while laying her on the bed next to Anna. "I'll be back shortly," he said as he bent to kiss Anna on the forehead.

Feeding twins was not something Anna had even thought to prepare for. Feeding one baby while another cried out in hunger broke her heart every time. The first few days were absolutely miserable, but soon enough, her routine with the babies worked itself out, and soon enough, Anna returned to helping out more around the house and with the other children. Beth had only been one for a few short months; now she was a big sister. Anna made certain to love on the sweet girl each and every day just as she had before. And other than stopping Beth from trying to play a little rough with the twins, all the children seemed to blend together perfectly.

Tommy could not have been more excited about having a new brother, and Mary had taken it upon herself to become the second little mother to the now three babies in the house. Emma had been Anna's saving grace up to this point. Miss Beth had started walking, or toddling was a better description, grabbing and tugging on everything she could get her hands on. The kitchen had quickly become a "not safe for Beth" room unless she was trapped in her high chair. However, her wooden spoon no longer gave her as much joy as it once had. So keeping her happy while strapped into her chair with old rags had become more of a challenge of late. "Ma, Ma, Ma, Ma!" Beth babbled from her spot on the floor while she played with a few homemade blocks.

Anna sat on the floor next to her while holding a fussing Oliver. "Hello, sweet girl, what should we build with those blocks you have there?"

Beth continued pounding two blocks together. Anna started stacking four of her own one on top of the other, then knocking it over. Beth giggled and started stacking a few of her own blocks to knock over. Anna sat with Beth playing until Oliver finally fell asleep tucked into her arm. "Okay, sweet girl, now it's time for your nap."

Standing up, she reached for Beth to tuck her into her one free arm. Just then, Seth came through the front door. "Well—" Then he stopped when he saw his wife's distressed look. "Oh," he said, lowering his voice, "I was going to tell you how nice it is for a man to walk into his home to a beautiful wife." Then he wiggled his eyebrows and gave her that grin that melted her into a puddle.

"It will only be nice," she whispered, "if these kids take a nap. I am exhausted." She smiled a small smile before stepping around him with one baby tucked into her elbow sound asleep, and one sitting perched on her hip.

"Lilly?" he asked.

"Emma was putting her down for me." She continued toward the stairs.

Seth cut her off with ease with one large step. "Let me rock her to sleep," he said, reaching for Beth. "You go take a nap with that big strong boy you have there."

Beth didn't hesitate and reached toward her father the moment he reached for her, slapping both of her hands against his cheeks.

"Come here, you. Let's go rock in your room for a few minutes, shall we?" he said in his daughter's ear as he held a hand out to Anna. "Come on now, Mrs. Hillard, I believe you need a nap as well," he said, right before capturing her lips with his. Then he smiled and waited for her to head up the stairs before him.

As soon as Anna's head hit her pillow, her body relaxed enough for her to close her eyes and sleep.

*****

When she woke, sometime later, Seth stood at the foot of the bed, bouncing a very upset little girl. "I wanted to let you sleep for as long as you could. Oliver is with Emma, but I imagine he will be just as angry as this one here soon," he whispered to his daughter, then kissed the top of her head before walking toward Anna.

Anna felt like a milk cow most days, the never-ending train of babies that needed to be fed. The doctor had checked in on the new babies just two weeks ago, telling her, "They look healthy enough, but because they were so small, they needed to be fed more often than a single baby."

Anna didn't think she could produce any more than she already was. She couldn't eat or drink enough without feeling like she had a hole in her foot, leaking it all out on the floor as she walked. The doctor would be here again today or tomorrow; she hoped she had exceeded his expectations. It was now almost March; the sun was shining a bit more each day. The winter had been pretty rotten, so sunshine was much needed. While the babies, all three of them, slept, she bundled herself up and sat on the porch swing. The fresh air was much needed as well, she thought to herself. She couldn't remember a time she had ever been more exhausted. Just sitting on the swing, she felt herself slip into a light slumber. The breeze on her face, the chill of the snow piled around the porch soothed her soul.

Seth watched Anna from the barn window as she slipped into oblivion; he needed to do more to help her. The babies demanded so much of her time, then Beth needed her. Mary and Tommy did their best to help, Emma was sent straight from heaven, but he was looking at a shell of his wife. Her cheeks had sunken in a bit more than he liked to see. When he would pull her close at night, her body felt way too light; she was always a whisper of a woman, now she was much less. He worried over her.

Jake and Emma had both talked to him in just the last week. The doctor had been zero help, telling her that because the babies were small, she wasn't feeding them enough. The babies were strong, and when he could, he would make them wait to eat a bit longer than the doctor had recommended if it meant Anna could sleep a bit longer. It was as if her body just couldn't keep up any longer, and she was wasting away before his very eyes.

He had pondered over everything he could possibly think of to help her, but so far, everything he had thought of hadn't helped. He prayed that when the good doctor came, either today or tomorrow, he would be bringing his latest attempt at helping his wife with him. He prayed again that he would, then he slipped out the door of the barn and headed to the porch. Once he reached the wood stairs, he carefully stepped up them, trying not to make much noise. Soon he was settling next to her on the swing, easing her into his arms. He would stay just like this forever if he needed to.

The doctor didn't make it today, so he will be by tomorrow, Anna thought to herself as she rocked Beth in her arms. Mary had Lilly on the floor, Tommy had Oliver on the couch, Seth read aloud out of the Bible on the couch next to Tommy. Emma sat in the chair next to Anna, and Jake stood behind her with his hands resting on the back. Anna's eyes wandered from face to face. Her family. Life was as perfect as she could have ever hoped for.

That night, Anna slept in peace; the babies slept for more than six hours. When Anna woke the next morning, she finally, for the first time in almost two months, felt refreshed.

Breakfast dishes had just been finished when the sound of voices could be heard coming up to the front door. *Who on earth?* Anna thought to herself. She picked up Lilly on her way out of the kitchen, headed toward the door when Seth walked in, then Dr. Richards, and a woman. Anna stopped, looking in Seth's direction, searching for answers. Then the woman lifted her head, her eyes locking with Anna's.

"Mama!" Anna whispered.

"Anna!" the woman said, rushing to her daughter and wrapping her arms around her, then she stepped back and looked down at the dark-haired baby in her daughter's arms. "And you must be Lilly." She hugged them both again, tears in both Anna and her mother's eyes.

"Mama, how did you know where to find me?" Tears rolled down her cheeks. "Harold"—the name stuck in her throat—"wouldn't let me write." Her voice cut off by the door opening. "Pa?" Confusion and joy bubbled out of Anna in a strange laugh mixed with a cry. "I cannot believe you are here," she said, shaking her head. "How?" She directed her question at Seth, who just smiled.

"It was easy. I put an advertisement in the newspaper that said, 'Looking for the parents of the most beautiful woman I know.'" He winked at her. "They," he said, pointing at her father then mother, "sent a letter. They knew it was you." The same strange sound escaped Anna as fresh tears streamed down her cheeks. "Had I known you would look at me the way you are right now, I would have done it sooner."

She rushed into his arms. "Thank you, Seth! You have brought me more joy than you will ever know!"

He kissed the top of her head. "You are welcome, sweetheart. Now let's go get your parents settled in so we can visit with them over lunch after we visit with the doctor."

"Oh yes, Dr. Richards, I am so sorry. I will go grab Oliver and meet you in the sitting room."

Emma had Oliver in the kitchen when Anna bounded through the door. "Oh, Emma, the greatest thing has just happened. My parents are here. They are truly here, Emma!" She reached for Oliver. "The doctor is also here to see these two little darlings."

Emma handed the baby over to Anna with a smile. "That they are, the two cutest little darlings I have ever seen."

Anna nodded in agreement. "Emma," Anna said as she headed back out the door, "would you please start something for lunch? Something special if you can."

Then she was gone again.

Seth had shown his in-laws to Emma's room, then excused himself to the sitting room to hear what the doctors had to say about the twins. He overheard the conversation before he entered the room. "Mrs. Hillard, you are definitely not feeding these babies enough. See? They are not growing as they should."

Seth stepped inside the room. "I don't mean to contradict a medical man, but how many sets of twins have you cared for over the years, Doc?" Seth said. "All Anna does all day is feed babies. I believe she is doing a fine job." He pointed at the children. "They are happy and healthy." He had finished walking into the room to stand next to his wife. "Anna is doing a great job, Doc. I wish you could see that."

Oliver started to fuss, and Anna reached for him, but Seth stopped her and grabbed his son. "Come here, little man, your pa will hold you so your ma's arms can have a break."

The doctor watched silently for a few seconds, then proceeded to check over Lilly. "Mrs. Hillard, you have been doing as good as any other new mother could. Just make sure you are feeding them both. It will be easy for one to get left behind." With that, the doctor picked up his bag and headed for the door. "I'll see myself out. Good day to ya, Hillard."

The front door opened, then clicked shut behind him. Anna stood, watching Seth as his eyes followed the doctor out the door; when his eyes returned to her, a smile spread across her face. She stepped toward him and wrapped her arms around his middle, pulling him close. "Thank you, Mr. Hillard." She leaned toward him.

"You're welcome, Mrs. Hillard," he said, then he kissed her, holding her face with his one free hand.

"I love you, Mr. Hillard," Anna said breathlessly.

"And I you, sweetheart." Then he kissed her again.

Lunch was served in the dining room; the whole family gathered around the table. Mary and Tommy had been taken with their new Grandpa and Grandma. Beth pounded away on her chair happily. Anna found out that Seth had reached out to her family before she had given birth to the babies. Unfortunately, the post was slow, and they had only received the letter last week. They packed up as soon as they could and headed west. It was past time for them to see their daughter. They had been shocked to hear of Harold's death, then Anna's new marriage to Seth. The fire and the birth of the babies rounded out the stories.

Seth excused himself to finish up some chores; Tommy followed close on his heels. Emma had made a pallet bed in Mary's room, so as soon as the dishes had been done, Emma headed up the stairs to finish up the arrangements. Anna and Ellen, her mother, headed into the sitting room with the three babies and Mary to chat and rock the babies to sleep. John, her father, headed out the door to help out with the chores and earn his keep. Anna couldn't believe everything she had missed in the last almost five years. She had received few letters from her parents since Harold had moved her to Montana. But now, talking to her mother, the few letters she had received had most likely been by accident. Harold had apparently not been giving them to her, for her mother said she had sent countless letters to her but had never received anything in return. Anna had only been allowed to write three letters to her parents in the three years she had been married; her parents had never received them, it seemed. Another one of Harold's ways to control her. She had begged her parents to come for her in her last letter to them. When she never heard back from them, she figured they were upset with her for marrying the man to begin with, so they had ignored her pleas for help. All along, they had been searching high and low for her.

When they received Seth's letter, claiming to be married to Anna, they left the next day to find her. Anna couldn't, but then she could believe this had all happened. Harold had been a monster; now looking into the face of her blonde-haired son, she couldn't imagine having children with anyone but Seth. How grateful she was that Harold had never fathered any of her children. Anna's brother Jacob was now married to a young woman named Patty, with a son just over a year old. Jacob had followed his dreams of becoming a writer for a newspaper in Chicago. Anna felt as though she was as new to her own family as the twins were in theirs. Five years had been too long. She had missed them all dearly.

Anna's parents stayed on the homestead for three weeks before they headed home to Ohio. Seth had promised to bring the family out to Ohio sometime in the next few years, once the twins could travel such a long distance. Anna and her mother had also promised to write to each other every week, never allowing so much time to be wasted. Watching the carriage roll down the cold hard road broke her heart in two. Now that she was a mother herself, she couldn't imagine not having her children close by. She vowed to herself to always keep her brood close.

Mary cried when her new grandparents left as well; the child had never had a grandparent before, so watching her new ones drive away broke her little heart. "Come, Mary, we will see them soon enough. Let's go inside and write a letter now so that it is waiting for them when they get home," Anna said, reaching for her daughter's hand, pulling her toward the door. That seemed to satisfy her for the moment; soon enough, she was sitting at the table in the kitchen with a cookie, a glass of milk, paper, and a pencil in hand.

Tommy sat in a chair, holding his little brother, telling him about all the fun adventures they would one day have. Anna stood at the stove, humming her favorite hymn, mixing the stew that Emma had started earlier. This beautiful woman, holding his newest daughter tucked under one arm, one daughter holding herself up by holding onto her mama's skirt, all the while Seth stood in the doorway, watching his family, thinking to himself, *God has blessed me beyond measure.*

Then he reached for Beth and snuggled her to his chest. Yes, God had blessed him.

About the Author

Aimee grew up in Utah, playing sports and running through fields as the family tomboy. As a high school senior, the thoughts of writing a book intrigued her. Unfortunately, it took twenty years for those thoughts to finally make their way to paper. In addition to finally writing, she is a wife, a mother to six children, a goat dairy farmer and works at a local greenhouse. She enjoys spending time with her family, running the family farm in the middle of nowhere, Idaho, and attending rodeos to watch her children compete in multiple events.